THE CHARLATAN

JOHN A. RUSSO

Burning Bulb
PUBLISHING

The Charlatan
by **John A. Russo**

Burning Bulb Publishing
P.O. Box 4721
Bridgeport, WV 26330-4721
www.BurningBulbPublishing.com

Cover designed by Gary Lee Vincent.

First edition.

Paperback edition ISBN 978-1-964172-05-7

CHAPTER 1

Dealey Plaza was the best novel I had ever written, but it sold fewer than five thousand copies in hardcover, and nobody wanted to follow up with a paperback release. It got good reviews in the *New York Times* and the *West Coast Review of Books* but got snidely dumped on in *Fangoria* and *Rue Morgue* by horror aficionados and wannabes who were affronted by my attempt to step outside of the genre. I tried to get the movie rights optioned but couldn't drum up any interest. Two big cardboard boxes, each containing one hundred hardcovers, were gathering dust in my basement.

"I did my best, David," my agent, Devin Lockhart, said. "I sent fliers and book trailers to the heads of all the acquisitions departments and pestered them till they stopped taking my phone calls. I couldn't budge them. Soon as they heard your name they'd say, David Cristi, he's that *horror guy,* isn't he?"

"Well, shit," I said, "I have more than one string to my bow. Like Albert Einstein."

"Strings to his bow?" said Devin, dropping his eyeglasses and letting them dangle on their gold chain. He was in his fifties, like me, but he looked younger because he dyed his hair and it hadn't receded as much as mine.

I said, "Einstein was a mathematical genius but also a damned fine violinist."

"No shit," Devin said, looking puzzled.

"He loved playing chamber music in his spare time with famous classical musicians. And they welcomed him because he was good."

"Well I'll be damned," said Devin. "No wonder he kept his hair wild and bushy."

"When I was a kid when my hair got too long my dad would tell me to get a violin instead of I needed a haircut."

Devin chuckled and I kept on ranting. "Why am I looked down on but Sam Raimi isn't? *The Evil Dead* got him his start but he doesn't make zombie films anymore, he gets to make what he *wants* to make. Mostly blockbuster comic book movies."

"You're pigeonholed, and somehow he isn't," Devin said. "But don't be so thin-skinned about it. Your movies won't ever win an Oscar or a Golden Globe, but they've made you rich. You don't have to try to turn yourself into the next Francis Ford Coppola."

"Then why did you tell me I should adapt *Dealey Plaza* into a screenplay?"

"Not the whole forty-some chapters, just the last hundred pages or so, concentrating on your main characters because they're utterly intriguing -- the tycoon who's running a pyramid scheme, the sexy young country singer, the badass FBI guy and the women's lib gal who reminds me of Gloria Steinem. But the trouble is, the novel starts out when they're in college and follows them for four decades and that's too much to cover, it makes the pace too slow. The theater owners want movies to be no longer than an hour and forty-five minutes, so there's a gap in between showings for the next audience to file in and buy popcorn. You should write a script that confines itself to the last six chapters of *Dealey Plaza* where they all go to their twenty-fifth college reunion and a sniper is fixing to gun them all down. You should also maybe change the title, call it *American Murders* or some such thing."

"Holy fuck, that's drastic!" I said. "It almost totally destroys my original intention."

"But once it's a hit you can mine it for prequels and sequels. You'll get the kind of respect you seem to crave, although I don't know why you have to crave it."

I couldn't get mad at Devin for being pragmatic. People who aren't in the movie business don't realize that selling a script to the studios isn't the first or even the biggest hurdle it faces. First it has to get accepted by a powerhouse agent like Devin Lockhart, who has the necessary clout. The agent and the buyers have to green light it before it will ever have a chance of reaching the theaters.

"Actually, I've started writing a movie version," I told Devin, just to show him I wasn't entirely immune to his way of thinking. "It starts off pretty much like Chapter One, but not so heavy on exposition. I think it works."

"Dump that idea," he said, adamantly shutting me down. "You do it the way I'm telling you and I promise I'll lay it on Max Parlin. I can get him to at least give it a read."

Perking up, I said, "You know Max personally?"

"Absolutely," said Devin. "When we did lunch the other day he said *The Mad Bomber* was a marketing man's wet dream, and we both laughed and bumped martini glasses."

"Yeah, he said that in *Hollywood Reporter* too. They gave it a big bold headline."

"That'll happen every time a script pulls down such big bucks," Devin said.

The Mad Bomber had been sold at auction for ten million plus points. It was about a global warming crusader who accuses fat-cats of getting rich by destroying the ozone layer, then goes nuts and starts sending them pipe bombs. Max Parlin was inspired to send copies of the screenplay and loudly ticking clocks in gift-wrapped packages addressed to the fat-cats of all the major studios. One of them tossed his package into an aquarium as soon as he heard it ticking, but when it didn't explode he fished it out and put in what turned out to be the winning bid. Two major stars promptly got signed and Clint Eastwood came on board to direct.

"Eastwood used to make spaghetti westerns," I said to Devin, "and look where he is now. I've got some P.T. Barnum in me, just like Max Parlin. When I four-walled my first slasher movie, I plastered the posters and trailers with fake blurbs that I wrote myself. Remember? I attributed them to reviewers and publications that didn't exist."

"Yeah, you even fooled *me,*" Devin said. "That took chutzpah. But now you want to move to a different level, and I think you can if you take my advice."

"I'm gonna do that," I promised. "Thanks for believing in me."

A few days later, he called me up and as soon as he heard my voice he said, "Are you working on it?"

"If you mean the *Dealey Plaza* thing, I've started writing it."

"Well, you already know what I'm going to tell you, but I'm going to say it anyhow. As you flesh out the script, keep some of your scintillating dialogue but not too much of it. Let the words and deeds of the characters speak for themselves. If all goes well, you'll be able to cast very fine actors and actresses who will make the movie come alive the way you want it to. You won't be working with shmucks who are already stars in their own minds."

Three months later I finished a first draft and Devin sent me notes for revisions. Then when I finished a second draft he sent it to Max Parlin. But after a two-week wait, we got a rejection slip, actually just a scrawl on a studio notepad, probably not even written by Max but by a secretary, claiming that although he very much admired *American Murders,* his plate was too full to take it on.

It was a bitter disappointment, but at this stage of my career I was thick-skinned enough to take heavy blows and still get up

6

every time I was knocked down, so I went back to making horror movies and building a solid stock portfolio.

Then, about ten years later, in July of 2003, I was sipping coffee on my patio when I got a call from Lance Goldman's secretary. "Hold for Mr. Goldman," she said, and he came on the line and said, "I wanna turn that book of yours into a miniseries. Nobody ever optioned it, did they?"

I said, "Which book?"

"*Dealey Plaza*. It's fucking great. Why didn't it ever get made?"

"Everybody assumed it was a rehashing of the Kennedy Assassination, which had already been done by Oliver Stone as a docudrama and wasn't any great shakes at the box office. That's probably why the Tom Brokaw quote on the cover of my book didn't impress anybody."

"What quote?"

"He said we were in a different country after those shots rang out in Dallas."

"Oh, well, I missed it if it was on the dust cover. My daughter's boyfriend got a copy signed by you, probably on eBay, and gave it to her for her birthday, and she gave it to me. I opened it up and got hooked. The main characters are fascinating and there's plenty of shoot-em-up, so I want to produce a pilot. Let's get in bed together on this, David."

I hated that expression *get in bed together* almost as much as I hated *Gore Master David Cristi*. But there seemed to be serendipity at work in the way my novel fell into Lance's hands. Studio bosses usually didn't want to read anything and they didn't want to get their hands dirtymaking movies; they only wanted to *distribute* movies because that's where the money is.

"You liked the novel?" I ventured to ask.

"Loved it," said Lance Goldman.

I halfway believed him so I said, "Let's talk further then."

"Are you in L.A.?"

"No, but I can be there. Give me a day or two to clear up a few things."

"Get back to me," he said.

I said, "Will do." But I didn't jump up and click my heels. I figured he'd try to lowball me with ten thousand or less for a one-year option. A few years ago I had pitched him on a horror comedy that I badly wanted to make, and he had let it slide without even calling me back. He ran Lance International Pictures as if he were an old-time Hollywood mogul, but the glory days of those legendary moguls were long gone. He was really only a big fish in his own pond, but he was swimming in dough from a string of action-hero movies starring a Rambo knockoff named Derrick Hubbara, who was a hair dresser and before that many other things before Lance "discovered" him while getting a shave and a manicure at Hubbara's salon. But Lance had to know that Hubbara wasn't the brightest light bulb on the planet, so I was stunned when he said, "Derrick Hubbara will direct."

I said, "Hold on, man. I don't think he has the chops."

"Then why did you use him in one of *your* movies, David?"

"I used him as an actor, not a director. Thanks to your *Scarifier* series, he has millions of fans . That's why I cast him, but I put him in a role I didn't think would hurt the movie. Frankly, his acting sucks."

"But he's a good director," Lance pounced.

"He gets along with the other actors, especially the young ladies, that's where his major focus always is, but onscreen he lacks a sharp sense of pacing and timing -- not to mention empathy."

"Then why do the fans love him?"

"I really don't know. Maybe for the same reason Jerry Lewis was a celebrated so-called genius in France -- but I can't

8

fathom whatever that reason is. In Hubbara's case I'd have to pin it on Hollywood hype, and you were the architect of that."

Hubbara had risen to box-office fame in *Scarifier Parts One, Two and Three.* Then Lance let him helm several episodes of a horror anthology, *Tales from the Bone Orchard,* that ran for three seasons on ABC. Even though he couldn't act, he had charisma and he played it to the hilt on the late-night talk shows hyping his latest movie as larger-than-life action hero Blaze Stewart who always wielded a powerful and stunningly accurate flame thrower to incinerate the bad guys and go out in a "blaze of glory." Gauche and tacky but the fans ate it up. So I had cast him in *Intensive Scare Part Four,* my own horror franchise, which I thought was superior to Lance's because my scripts had more to them than just blood and gore and fiery carnage.

I said, "Come on, Lance, do you really believe Hubbara has the skills a good director *needs to* have? I know he doesn't have them as an actor. Anytime I wanted to try something inventive, he'd fight me until I made him think it was his own idea. Then I had to grin and clench my teeth while he bragged on it in the screening room when he saw how well it worked."

"Okay, he's a prima donna," Lance admitted. "But I saw that movie you put him in, and the two of you pulled off some real magic."

"The magic mostly came from me," I said, sticking up for myself.

"Well, look," Lance said. "You and Derrick have a lot in common, both being from Pittsburgh. I think we should shoot our pilot mostly there, and in West Virginia, where that wild-ass fight between the big coal miner and the singer's husband takes place. Do you have a good contact for getting us some Pennsylvania film tax credits?"

"I do," I said. "That's why I shot *Intensive Scare Part Four* mostly utilizing Pittsburgh locations."

9

"Let's not look a gift horse in the mouth, then," Goldman said. "Do you agree?"

"On locations but not on Hubarra," I said, and I went on to insist that if a movie version of my best novel was finally going to be made, the last thing I wanted was a hack calling the shots behind the camera.

However, it became a moot point because three weeks later Lance Goldman was murdered, and all the assets of Lance International Pictures got tied up in probate and once again *Dealey Plaza* did *not* get made, and I was forced to contemplate the wisdom and the mockery of an ancient proverb: *Man plans and the gods laugh.*

CHAPTER 2

The murder of Lance Goldman wasn't the first murder in my life. When I was thirteen years old, the naked, mutilated bodies of my best friend, Ron Demick, and two of our classmates were found floating in a muddy pond. While I was overwhelmed with the grief and terror it caused me, three gangbangers who called themselves Satanists and constantly picked on me and Ron were convicted and sent to prison, where they served seventeen years till DNA exonerated them. The grief and terror resumed in full force. Over the next twenty years, I was still having horrific recurrent nightmares, so I pleaded with the original investigator, Vito Martinelli, to reopen the case, and together we finally succeeded in unmasking the real killer. It had long been one of the most maddening of cold cases, hashed and rehashed on true-crime TV, and the solving of it made it even more sensational. A publisher talked me into writing a book about it which became a best-seller and gave me a degree of mainstream notoriety that I had never before attained as a movie director.

In the midst of all that hoopla, people started seeking me out and coaxing me to do something about their own unsolved cases. They seemed to think I might be able to work wonders where law enforcement had failed. I didn't believe I was endowed with any miraculous abilities but what I *could* do was turn their cases over to Vito Martinelli. Thanks to the notoriety of the Ronald Demick case, Vito was now in high demand as a private investigator and my daughter Joy was working for him, with the goal of obtaining her P.I. license. I got drawn into several of the cases I brought to them, partly because I wanted to stay close to Joy and protect her if need be, even though I didn't have full confidence in my ability to do so. Because of all that, getting entangled in the murder of Lance Goldman was an easy trap for me to fall into. I had always despised murderers and had suffered in grief and misery for years because of what had been done to Ron Demick and my two other childhood pals. Lance Goldman and I weren't friends except on a business, not a deeply personal level, but his murder had changed my life almost as dramatically as Ron's had, by putting the kibosh to an aspiration that for a long time had been a focal point of my career.

I had never met Lance's widow, Veronica, but she phoned me just two days after the discovery of her husband's badly charred body and that of his chauffeur in a burnt-out limousine. She began by haltingly introducing herself, then apologetically informed me that Lance's closed-casket memorial service would be attended only by a few people in the immediate family and I should not feel slighted for not receiving an invitation. Then she got to the real point of her phone call. She said she wanted to hire Vito Martinelli to help bring the murderer to justice because she had no confidence that the Pittsburgh police knew what they were doing.

"They really are highly competent," I told her. "Vito is in touch with friends of his from before he became a private investigator, and he told me Lance's case is top priority. They aren't leaving a stone unturned."

"But I just spoke with Sheriff Boyce and got told there's nothing to report," Veronica spouted angrily. "He sounded embarrassed at his lack of progress. But he may've been stone-walling me. "

I said, "He probably hasn't had any sleep since he got called out on this. He knows full well that any case that doesn't get solved within forty-eight hours usually goes cold, so he's under a lot of pressure."

Veronica jumped right in on that, quite adamantly saying, "That's why I want to hire your close associate, Mr. Martinelli. I'll never forgive myself if I don't do everything I can for Lance. He was a tough businessman but a kind and loving father and husband."

I was somewhat surprised to hear hard-nosed Lance spoken of so fondly by his spouse, but I was also touched by it. "I'll talk to Vito," I promised her. "You can rest assured that either he or I will get back to you."

"How soon? I hope you won't leave me hanging."

"Don't worry," I told her. "Your husband was very important to me."

There was a long pause and I could feel her mistrust filling the air.

"And he still is," I added. "You have my condolences."

"Thank you," she said with a lack of warmth. Then she said goodbye and ended the call.

Before I phoned Vito, the lead-up to Lance Goldman's murder tormented me anew. He likely was being killed and then crudely and callously cremated at the same time that Derrick Hubarra and I were waiting for him at the Pittsburgh Hilton, so we could discuss the locations we had intended to start scouting the following day. Utterly flummoxed as to why he would suddenly become a no-show, we tried to track him down by using his pager and messaging him over and over on his cell phone, but nobody in his office back in L.A. was able to tell us anything helpful. We went to the registration desk and found out that he hadn't yet checked into the hotel, so we waited in one of the restaurants, constantly checking back at the desk for the next three hours. Then we went to the Public Safety Building and filed a Missing Person Report. We had to spend the next two days totally in the dark. Finally on the third day Hubarra phoned me sounding like he was crying. "They found him," he blurted through sobs. "He's dead. Oh, God, it's horrible!"

Images of what had happened to Ron Demick flashed through my mind unbidden and I wondered if whatever had been done to Lance Goldman could be any worse than that.

Struggling to pull himself together, Hubarra said, "I think detectives are coming here any minute. I'm sure they're gonna want to talk to you as well."

I turned on the TV in my family room, channel-surfed for news reports, and learned some sketchy details. A limousine had been found in an empty warehouse with two blackened, shriveled bodies inside. They were burned beyond recognition but presumed to be "the remains of movie mogul Lance Goldman and his driver." The torched limousine was a blackened and twisted skeletal vestige of itself, but a VIN number had been readable, which had enabled it to be ascertained as the vehicle that had been sent to pick up Mr. Goldman at the Greater Pittsburgh International Airport. So far there were no readily discernible leads and no obvious motive, but Allegheny County Sheriff Herbert Boyce said in an interview clip that he was confident the murderer or murderers would be caught and punished. "Once we discover the motive, it will lead us to the killer," the sheriff asserted. "Our investigation is just beginning. But I assure you that something will point us in the right direction."

I didn't know how he could assure anybody of anything at this point, so I figured he was trying to scare the culprit or culprits and shake something loose. However, two days after the discovery of the bodies, it seemed that the investigation was stalled. Derrick Hubbara and I both had been interviewed but not harshly grilled, and there was no indication that either of us was being considered as a suspect or a person of interest. I kept doggedly following the news reports but learned little more as the Goldman murder quickly dropped out of the headlines.

Then came the phone call from Victoria Goldman. And when it ended, I spent a few minutes contemplating what I would say to Vito. I was pretty sure he would want to take the case on, and so would Joy. It was certainly high profile and there was the added enticement that it would be powered by Goldman International's big bucks.

CHAPTER 3

"The wire came in," Joy said, coming into Vito's conference room.

"The full advance?" he asked.

"Yep, twenty-five thousand," she said with her usual bright smile.

"Sit down and eat, honey," I suggested. I was sitting opposite Vito and our massive Primanti's sandwiches were laid out on wax paper in front of us. Joy sat down in front of hers and stared at it for a long moment without unwrapping it, then said, "You know I can never eat more than half of one."

The original Primanti Brothers was in Pittsburgh's produce center, and forty years ago I first became acquainted with it and loved going there. The two dark, balding, Italian immigrant brothers who owned the place ran around shouting and cursing at one another constantly, an integral part of the fun for the packed house of truckers, masons, carpenters, plumbers and assorted other kinds of roughnecks who smiled, chuckled and guffawed, gruffly enjoying the camaraderie. I loved Pittsburgh's ethnic bars and neighborhoods and it was partly why I still lived in a nearby suburb long after I had acquired agents in New York and Los Angeles. I let them make the deals where money was unreal and spent it back home where it was more of a commodity that I understood.

The *Famous Primanti Brothers Sandwiches*, as the menu dubbed them, consisted of the customer's choice of beef, fish, hot sausage, sweet sausage or any of a dozen other main choices, each piled high with cole slaw and French fries and

16

slathered with vinegar and oil dressing, all of it crushed between two thick slices of crusty Italian bread. You could even ask for your sandwich to be piled between two heels of bread if you wanted to, but then it would be three or four inches thick and very hard for your mouth to open wide enough. The original Primanti Brothers was still where it had first started out, but over the years it had transmogrified into a chain with modern outlets, far less colorful than the original, in multiple locations, including inside the Steeler and Pirate stadiums.

Taking occasional sips of Pepsi to help me deal with my preposterously thick sandwich, I asked, "How soon are we gonna have a look at the warehouse?"

"Right away," Vito responded. "But it's not the only crime scene. The two vics must've been kidnapped either right at the airport or someplace in between. They were driven into the warehouse and shot, or maybe shot on the way there, then they were soaked with gasoline and torched, limo and all, which tells us we can rule out a carjacking. If the car was the objective, it'd already be in Mexico. Goldman was meant to die and the chauffeur was collateral damage."

Joy said, "So we have to hope we can find a keen-eyed witness or maybe video surveillance from the airport or close to it, right Vito?"

He said, "Absolutely."

He and I were both wearing dark suits with white shirts and monochromatic neckties in case we had to try to gain cooperation from somebody without having badges to flash. Joy always looked good enough to wheedle information out of anybody, but today she was going to hold down the office while Vito and I were out gallivanting. I couldn't look at her without feeling a twinge of fatherly pride. A perky ash blonde, she was wearing designer jeans, a long-sleeved blue and green silk blouse, a thin gold necklace and tiny gold earrings. She

17

had gotten divorced a year ago and was back to enjoying the single life, free of a domineering ex-husband and not under her father's wing anymore. She was living in her own apartment and liking it that way.

She asked Vito, "Any chance the warehouse has CCTV?"

"No," he said, "because that'd be too damned easy. I already talked to Sheriff Boyce from down there. I reminded him of who we are and he remembered us right away from the Roland Fornier case, so he's willing to let us into the warehouse. He's gonna stick with us, though, to make sure we don't disturb any evidence."

"He remembers us from that case and yet he doesn't trust you?" Joy said, pursing her lips indignantly and making her dimples stand out.

"We're not exactly buddy, buddy," Vito told her. "He has a job to protect, so he can divulge some things but he can't confide in me as if I'm still a cop. At this point we're not even sure who he might have questioned other than Derrick Hubbara and your dad. I asked Veronica Goldman if she gave Sheriff Boyce any specific leads, anybody she could think of who might have held a grudge against her husband, and she emailed me the same five names she gave him. They're all people in the movie business -- three females and two men. Two of the women filed charges against Lance for sexual harassment seven or eight years ago and the charges were dismissed after they were paid off. If they didn't get the big bucks they were after, they could have a revenge motive."

"How might we pursue that?" I asked him.

"Joy is already on it, utilizing public records and court records, I mean the ones that haven't been sealed. While you and I are tracing the possible abduction route to the arson scene, she's going to stay here engulfing herself in painstaking research. Right, Joy?"

18

"Right, boss," she answered half flippantly because she preferred field work to office work, as Vito and I well knew. Pushing her chair back, she said, "I can't eat another bite. We should've split two of these sandwiches instead of ordering one apiece. To tell you the truth, I really prefer just one slice of their thin-crust pizza or a cup of their 'Almost Famous Chili' with Italian bread and butter instead of plain old crackers."

"I'll keep that in mind, but I like *all* their stuff," Vito said, finishing his last bite and balling up his messy and sopping wax paper.

I said, "I don't think the county cops up here are done with me or Derrick. They know that we knew where Lance was supposed to be, his whole itinerary as a matter of fact, so we were perfectly situated to set up an ambush."

"That's why both of you are on Veronica's list," Vito said. "I've got to vet both of you thoroughly enough that she'll become a believer. However, let me point out that you may actually know something you're not fully aware of. Or you may be able to get Hubbara to reveal things he won't readily reveal to the cops, or to me when I confront him. So I'd like you to get in touch with him and pump him as much as you can. Try to find out if he suspects anyone we might not think of. Let him know I'm on the case and Veronica is my client, which will ramp up the pressure on him. Get him to come in here for a face to face. Unlike the cops, I can't compel it, but Veronica can, assuming he still wants to star in more movies for Lance International Pictures."

"Remember, I cast him in one of *my* pictures, Vito. He might want to suck up to me in hopes I'll cast him in another one. Either him or his daughter."

"His daughter?" Joy said, casting a surprised look at me.

"Jennifer Huber, that's Derrick's teenaged kid," I told her. "She can't act any better than he can, but of course I would never say it publicly. She's only fourteen and has a lot to learn, so maybe she'll get better."

"I know who you mean now," said Joy. "Jenny Huber. She's in that TV series called *Zombie Hunterz*. Isn't it from Lance International?"

"Right, honey," I said. "You've watched it?"

"I never heard of it," Vito said dismissively.

Joy said, "I was flipping through channels one day and scoped maybe fifteen minutes of it, till it broke for commercials. It's mild zombie fun for school kids. The young actors and actresses get to defeat zombies using whips, judo and martial arts sort of stuff. There's a lot of action, but it's as bloodless as TV wrestling."

I said, "When I cast Derrick in my last movie, he wanted me to write his daughter into the script. But I refused."

Joy said, "Good for you, Dad."

"Not only that," I said, " but I took a look at some of her clips on YouTube, and that's why I know she can't act."

Vito thought for a moment, then said, "Is there any chance that somebody might've killed Lance Goldman to stop the *Dealey Plaza* pilot from happening? Veronica told me Lance International Pictures is being pitched on a slate of other projects now that *Dealey* is a no-go. Could that be a viable motive, in your opinion?"

"I really doubt it. But crazier things have happened in the movie biz."

Vito stood up and said, "Okay, enough banter for now. Let's head to the airport."

CHAPTER 4

Vito and I rode in his black Cadillac for twelve miles on Route 51 South, then bypassed the Liberty Tunnels and took the ramp onto Route 376 toward the airport for another eight miles. It was a sunny day in mid April, chilly outside but hot in the car till we turned up the air conditioning. Palm Sunday and then Easter Sunday had gone by already. I informed Vito that Lance had wanted to get all the religious holidays, including Passover, behind us before flying here to scout locations.

"Was he a practicing Jew?" Vito asked.

"Don't really know but I don't think so. Seems like most people I know these days are closet atheists."

"I sort of still believe," he said, "but not fanatically. You don't believe in any of it, do you?"

"Not really. By the time I got rid of the guilt trips I was no longer very Catholic."

"Then who will you thank if you ever get an Oscar?" he said drolly.

"Nobody up in the sky, that's for sure. I don't believe my mom and dad are looking down at me either. Or *up* at me, which would've been the case with my father."

Vito chuckled as he pulled into valet parking. The plan was to meet the sheriff in the passenger pickup area, which had its usual line-up of taxis and shuttles. Vito had kept in touch with Sheriff Boyce by cell phone, alerting him to our ETA, so he showed up promptly and we jumped into the black, yellow and white County Sheriff Department vehicle that he was driving. Vito got into the front passenger seat and I got in back, behind the sheriff. As we had told Joy, we were acquainted with him from a case we had worked two years ago that had led us into his county. He was wearing his brown campaign hat, dark brown trousers and a tan uniform shirt with dark brown epaulettes.

As he pulled out, he said to Vito, "Like I told you, we got a tip shortly after the Missing Person Report hit the news. The tipster caught the report on an overhead monitor as he was heading toward baggage claim, and he punched nine-one-one while he was waiting for his wife to pick him up like I picked up you guys. He said he was pretty sure he saw Lance Goldman getting into a black limo while a chauffeur took his luggage, tossed it in and slammed the doors. But that's all the witness saw. He couldn't tell us where the limo headed after it got on the exit ramp."

"How was he so sure he saw Lance Goldman?" Vito asked. "Lance was a movie producer, not an actor -- how many people could recognize him so easily?"

Sheriff Boyce said, "Last year Goldman was a celebrity guest at a media convention in Monroeville, where *Dawn of the Dead* was filmed, and our guy said he saw him give a talk there 'cause he was with his son, who wants to be a filmmaker."

"Oh, yeah," I said. "It's called Living Dead Weekend. I would've been there, but I was at a similar event in England."

"Anyhow, the witness was there and so was Lance Goldman," the sheriff said. "His photo was on their web page. The witness had given us a good lead but it was also a needle in a haystack. We had to seek out all the video surveillance footage we could gather from nearby gas stations, convenience stores or whatever in a couple-mile radius on all possible routes from the airport to somewhere, but we didn't know where. I knew from the Missing Person Report that he hadn't made it to the hotel, so I took a couple of big chances that didn't focus on Pittsburgh proper. I sent a couple of my guys north, toward

22

Erie, and I headed south with one of my deputies, toward Washington."

Vito and I both knew he didn't mean Washington, D.C. but Washington, Pennsylvania, which was often called Little Washington. We were about forty-five miles from it and heading there made me uneasy. It was a hub of Klan and neo-Nazi activity.

"I'm not gonna let you guys flounder like we had to," Sheriff Boyce said. "I'll take you directly to where we found the torched limo with the bodies in it to save you all the backtracking and false steps we had to take before we finally got lucky."

"Why did you have to go through all that?" Vito said. "I thought all the limo companies had GPS monitoring built into their automobiles."

"Some of them do, but this one didn't. We found out when we zeroed in on a limo service paid for with a Lance International credit card."

For some time now, we had been driving through rural farmland without encountering very many small commercial enterprises. And when the ramp toward Little Washington came up, he took it to where he had to stop for a stop sign that was bent and twisted by several shotgun pellets and bullet holes. "Here's where we had to pick from two intersecting two-lane blacktops," he said. "Eeny, meeny, minee, mo...and I chose the one that was a total dud. No stores, no closed-circuit surveillance cameras on any of the barns or farmhouses, no sign of a black limo. So, I backtracked and the other road paid off. But at first, I cussed it out because we found only one little gas station that had cameras, one outside over the entrance, and another one above the counter when we went in. The clerk scrolled through all the captured stuff for us -- and I almost shouted hooray when we actually caught a quick glimpse of the limo flashing by. But where the hell did it go? There was no way of knowing. But then I thought of something. You want to take a guess?"

I had a glimmer, not even strong enough to be called a hunch, and I didn't feel I ought to pipe up about it. Vito didn't say anything either.

The sheriff said, "You guys remember that kids' game where the leader tells the other kids they're getting warm when they're closer to where he's got something hidden?"

"I think I know what you hit on," Vito said.

Sheriff Boyce said, "You *both* ought to know. A kidnapping and a murder brought you down here a couple years ago."

"The Aryan Confederacy," I muttered finally.

"That's what *I* was thinking," said Vito. "I hope we're not dealing with *those* assholes again."

"Me, too," said the sheriff. "The reason I thought of them, I had to ask myself why the hell would that limo be down here? What were they going to do with their wealthy high-profile hostage if he wasn't dead yet and they were intent on holding him for ransom? They wouldn't want to keep taking chances out in the open in this part of rural America where a sleek black limousine might as well be sporting a red flag. I tried to imagine where they might hide it, and that's when I pictured the deserted neo-Nazi compound. Most of it was razed to the ground after those nut cases were shot or captured, but a corrugated-steel building was left standing after a cache of military surplus stuff was emptied out of it and burned in a pit."

I dreaded being anywhere close to what used to be a neo-Nazi fortress. Two years ago I almost got killed by a demented renegade of the Aryan Confederacy who had kidnapped the granddaughter of one of my lifelong pals. I wasn't anxious to have another run-in with their ilk in any way, shape or form. I had thought I had closed that chapter of my life, and now it seemed that perhaps I hadn't. But I had to buck up in front of Vito and the sheriff.

After we turned off of the blacktop onto a dirt road through the woods, we came upon a bullet-pocked concrete bunker, which gave me a twinge of past fear, but I was consoled by the fact that the steel chain-link fence topped with razor wire was gone. No sentries, no lookout towers. We drove unimpeded up to the corrugated steel building the sheriff had reminded us of, and I stepped on scraps of new-looking yellow-and-black crime scene tape partly embedded in yellow dirt. The day was a lot warmer now that the sun had been out for a while, as the sheriff led me and Vito up to the padlocked door.

"Are we gonna be able to see in there?" Vito asked the sheriff, noting that the huge steel building had no windows.

"Once we get inside there's a double-wide load-in door that has a pull-rope like a regular garage door," Sheriff Boyce said. "To your point, there's no electricity so we'd need to have a generator going to get the door to go up easier. We had generator-powered lights when we documented the burn scene, but they're no longer here. But the pull rope makes the big door go up pretty easy because it's on a gear system that must've been designed for easy operation."

"I'm dying to pull on it," Vito quipped sardonically.

"It's like using a lat machine," said the sheriff. "You look plenty strong enough to pull a helluva stack of twenty-five-pound plates."

"Looks are deceiving," said Vito. "I'm outta shape."

Taking a key with a tag on it out of his pants pocket, Sheriff Boyce said, "This is for the new padlock we put on. The perps must've used bolt cutters on the old one 'cause it was lyin' in pieces on the ground. I bagged it and had it dusted for fingerprints and we didn't find any."

He used the key and I hung back, a little behind Vito, as the door swung open and a repulsive odor of melted metal, burnt paint, burnt plastic, burnt fabric and burnt rubber wafted out, along with the appalling odor of burnt human flesh. I was relieved that the torched limousine wasn't in there anymore, and of course neither were the torched bodies, but it was still a realm of death. I could've damned near choked to death on the odors.

Sheriff Boyce led the way to the double-wide door at the end of the building where a thick bull rope was hanging down. He hauled on it, putting forth substantial effort, and sure enough the door went up, letting in enough sunlight for us to see better and to feel a little less claustrophobic.

"That's where it was," Sheriff Boyce said, pointing to a huge blotch of discolored and fire-crumbled concrete, a macabre blotch about twelve feet long and eight feet wide.

"Can't miss it, can you?" Vito murmured without expecting an answer.

"I've seen a lot of disgusting things but this ranks close to the top," the sheriff said. "Not so much now but the first time we were in here. Made my stomach do flips. I didn't have any Vicks to rub on my mustache." He shook his head somberly.

I stared at the limo-sized blotch on the dark gray concrete floor and at the swastikas, Heil Hitlers and bloody hearts and daggers spray-painted on a wall a few feet from the ugly, filthy- looking blotch. Then I let my eyes wander upwards to the steel beams and girders, which were dusty, dirty and marred in places by black, greasy smoke.

Sheriff Boyce said, "I'm going out and smoke a cigar. Call me back in if you think of any questions."

Vito had started pacing around slowly, eyeing everything with the trained eyes of a seasoned detective, so I followed him without fastening on anything I could call a clue. After about ten minutes of that, we went out and joined the sheriff who carefully stubbed out what was left of his cigar on the side of the windowless steel siding and put it in a baggy, then into his breast pocket.

"I don't smoke cheap ones," he said. "Gotta save 'em for later when they're this long, even though I don't smoke 'em too often. Well, you had your look, Vito. I don't think me and my guys missed anything of evidentiary importance. Do you?"

"Nope. And I didn't expect that you would have," Vito said.

"We took a raft of photos while the bodies were still here in the limo and you're welcome to look at 'em. I brought a packet of 'em and they're in my briefcase. Let's stop somewhere and have coffee and a sandwich and you can shuffle through them."

"I'm not going to look at them," I said. "If I did, I wouldn't be able to eat. Vito can take stuff like that better than I can."

"We can't take it either," Sheriff Boyce said. "But we force ourselves to do it."

We piled back into the sheriff's vehicle and remained silent for a while. Then, as we left the former compound and got back onto asphalt, Vito said, "I don't necessarily buy that this case has anything to do with the Aryan Confederacy or what's left of it."

I was surprised to hear him say that because of the fact that Lance Goldman was a Jew and a wealthy motion picture producer and the anti-Zionist conspiracy nuts fanatically spouted a lot of crap about how the Jews owned Hollywood and used to it churn out propaganda for Israel and for the Worldwide Deep State.

"You know what? I don't tend to buy it either, in terms of the Aryan Confederacy, that is," Sheriff Boyce said.

Vito said, "It's too pat. I think I smell a set-up. I wouldn't hang my hat on it, but I think there here might be some other motive at work here.

CHAPTER 5

Joy joined me and Vito for breakfast at the Blue Flame, which had been a landmark eatery on Route 51 South, just outside of Clairton, ever since I was a little boy. It was a large, brightly lit establishment, nothing fancy about it, but neat and clean to a fault, and its simple homespun meals were better than most moms could -- or would -- cook nowadays, which made me think of something said by Henry J. Heinz back in the nineteenth century: "If you do a common thing uncommonly well, success will surely follow." The "common thing" that he did so well was making ketchup and pickles that were better than everybody else's, which had made him a Pittsburgh legend. One day when we were watching a Steelers game at our American Legion post Vito got a big laugh out of the bar crowd by telling them that wide receiver Hines Ward didn't need to play football because he was heir to the Montgomery Ward and H.J. Heinz fortunes.

Vito had a droll and churlish sense of humor that was hard to figure out sometimes. He had *Victor Martin Associates* stenciled in black and gold letters on the glass door to his office even though there was no Victor Martin and there were no associates. When I asked him why, he said, "I want to look Waspish in the Yellow Pages so I can reel in some of the fat cats who're prejudiced against dagos."

"But they'll soon find out your real name, won't they?" I asked him teasingly.

"Too late once I've cashed their non-refundable retainers," he answered.

The Blue Flame had a couple of cute young waitresses, but several had been there for decades and looked like kindly grandmas. The tables were full but one of the grandmas showed us to an empty booth and we leafed through extra-large menus replete with laminated photos of breakfast, lunch or dinner items served all day long, bacon and eggs, grits, home fried with peppers and onions, frittata, sandwiches and wraps, meatloaf and mashed potatoes, fried chicken, grilled pork chops, and much more. But we didn't waver from the fact that we were there for breakfast, and after one of the grandmas took our orders, Vito and I filled Joy in on our findings in Little Washington, then she handed us print-outs of her research on the five persons of interest provided by Veronica Goldman, and we set the documents aside so they wouldn't get food smears on them when we started to eat.

Joy said, "I summarized everything I could find out from public records, like newspaper and magazine articles and interviews and bios and credits on *IMDb*."

"What's that?" Vito asked.

"The *International Movie Data Base*. Everyone in the biz is on it. It's all good background stuff that we should acquaint ourselves with before doing in-person interviews -- that is, if any of them will actually talk to us."

"You're right," I said, "The ones who settled their claims against Lance Goldman will probably fall back on their nondisclosure agreements, and there's not much we can do about it."

Vito said, "According to his wife, they were all settled. I don't think he had anything pending."

"Dad, do you think Lance really did those things?" Joy asked. "You knew him pretty well, didn't you?"

"Not all that well, honey. But for what it's worth he didn't strike me as a womanizer. He thought of himself as a mogul of

29

sorts, and I think most of his energy went into the distribution and marketing of his movies."

"But that leaves plenty of time for sex -- in any man's life," Vito said with a churlish look on his face. "Did you know that the average duration of a sex act is only nine minutes?"

"Not if you do it right," I quipped back at him.

"Dad!" Joy chided, but with a barely repressed smile on her face.

"Well, I read it somewhere," said Vito.

I said, "Where? On the *Hustler* website?"

Joy said, "Come on, guys, let's get serious. How're we going to make Victoria's suspects talk to us?"

Vito flashed a grin and said, "Time for me to stop holding back on the two of you. I've been itching to tell you we're no longer up shit creek without a paddle. Sheriff Boyce phoned me last night to suggest swearing me in as one of his deputies. He says he doesn't have the budget or the manpower to handle a two-pronged investigation, both in his jurisdiction where the crime took place and in Los Angeles county where it may have its roots."

"That's *great* news!" Joy exclaimed.

"Yep," said Vito with his charming brand of smugness. "It's a good thing I stayed clean

when I was a cop. I was tempted to go dirty, but I didn't. Some of the guys who did went to jail. They took payoffs from pimps and street walkers and joints with poker machines. Sheriff Boyce would rather swallow glass than deputize a PI, but he seems to trust me, maybe because we worked with him so well a couple years ago. He told me his CSI people have been sifting through piles of ashes and burnt plastic for the past few days and they found what was left of the murder weapon -- and guess what? It's a Luger. The grips are burned off and the barrel is half melted but there's enough left to tell it was a

Luger. So that adds to the Aryan Confederacy angle if there really is one -- which I doubt."

I said, "I'm guessing there isn't enough left to do a ballistics test."

"Unfortunately not," Vito acknowledged. "Bullet fragments were recovered since both victims were shot in the head. The slugs didn't go through and through because they had to pass through bone, which caused them to be too fragmented to be of forensic value."

"Shit," Joy murmured softly.

Vito said, "Sheriff Boyce also told me that a canvass of the passenger lists on recent flights from L.A. to Pittsburgh failed to turn up any of the five names on Victoria's list. I don't think any of them would risk using phony ID's because passports and drivers licenses are so carefully scrutinized these days, ever since nine eleven."

We sipped coffee and thought things over for a while.

Breaking the silence, I said, "l have a bit of good news. I'll be with Derrick Hubbara this weekend at the Pittsburgh Horror Festival. We're both featured guests. We'll be signing autographs and doing Q&A's all three days, but I'll make sure to bump into him during the off hours."

"Good," said Vito. "Maybe you'll get something out of him. He's so full of himself he might let something slip."

I realized that although Vito had only met Derrick briefly at the Pittsburgh Oscar Party last year, he had accurately sized him up.

Our meals arrived: a stack of buttermilk pancakes with real maple syrup for Vito, and eggs sunny side up with sausage links, hash browns and sourdough toast for me and Joy. I often cooked the same kinds of offerings at home, and I was a pretty good cook, but why did the Blue Flame always seem to do it better? We dug in zestfully after our grandmotherly waitress freshened our coffee.

31

Vito wiped his mouth and said to Joy, " When we get back to the office, book a flight for you and me for early tomorrow morning. Phone Victoria Goldman and tell her to have a driver meet us when we land at LAX."

"What about me?" I said. "Shouldn't I go too? I'm the one who knows Hollywood."

"I think we'll be there for several days," Vito answered. "So you can stay here and ply Hubbara for whatever you can get out of him, then you can join us in L.A. For the time being, we're gonna have a three-pronged, not just a two-pronged, investigation -- Sheriff Boyce in Washington County, you here in Pittsburgh and me and Joy on the West Coast. We ought to accomplish *something*."

"One would hope so," I said.

Joy said, "Dad? Why do you sound so low key?"

"Because we don't really have anything to hang our hats on."

She said, "You're too pessimistic."

I said, "You know as well as I do that when an investigation starts out you have to wonder if you're going to actually solve it or if it's going to turn into a cold case in spite of your best efforts."

"Well, *I* think we're going to solve it!" she said with her usual perkiness.

"Attagirl," said Vito.

I said, "I'll feel a lot better once we get more of a handle on things."

"Relax. That's going to happen," said Vito.

On the several murder cases that he and I had become involved with, I had tried to be an optimist and a pragmatist at the same time, which was the same way I approached movie projects. The trick was to not be self-defeating but to maintain a pitch of enthusiasm that could carry the cast, crew and investors that I needed right along with me, while at the same time being able to inwardly realize that it could all come crashing down and amount to nothing, as had happened to the *Dealey Plaza* project as a result of Lance's murder.

Thinking of that snake-bitten project made me think of my agent, Devin Lockhart, and I said, "I'm gonna run the names Joy did her research on past my agent. Devin knows just about everybody and everything that goes on in Hollywood. He phoned me and said his condolences about Lance, and that's as far as it went. But maybe he knows some dirt that he's holding back, maybe even a suspect that he can point us to."

"Good thinking," said Vito.

"See, Dad? You're getting into it," Joy said.

CHAPTER 6

The Pittsburgh Horror Festival was held in a huge vacant section of Monroeville Mall, which used to be state-of-the-art. It was first built about forty years ago, and in the early 1980's *Dawn of the Dead* was filmed there, but these days large sections were going unoccupied and this made the site cheap enough for a weekend rental by the promoters. Thanks to the films of George A. Romero, Russ Streiner and John Russo, Pittsburgh was known as The Zombie Capital of the World, and each June the Horror Festival was attended by thousands of psyched-up fans, which made it one of the largest events of its type in the nation. I seldom missed it when I was in town. I liked talking shop with my friends in the biz, hobnobbing with my fans and partying with them in the upscale bars and restaurants nearby.

The show opened at five PM on Friday, so I got there at two in order to have enough time to load my stuff in and set up my tables, then mingle a little bit with the other celebrities who were also busy setting up. Two heavily bearded staff volunteers wearing red T-shirts with black and red zombie logos on their fronts and STIFF rather than STAFF on their backs helped me load in and showed me to my ten-by-ten booth, which sported a four-foot by three-foot banner that said DAVID CRISTI in big bold red letters above a montage of scary images from my movies. They offered to help me set up, but I declined, trying not to abuse their enthusiasm by apologetically saying, "I have a one-track mind and it's easier and faster if I think it out and do it myself rather than trying to tell someone else what to do

34

when I'm not even sure yet." They still seemed uncertain so I asked them to stop by later and I'd give them each a signed poster.

Derrick Hubbara had a booth similar to mine across the room from me, and I saw that he was already almost completely set up and ready for customers. On either side of us were eight celebrity booths facing outward from each opposing wall, with a wide-open space in between, outfitted with stanchions and velvet ropes to facilitate crowd control and accommodate lines of fans anxious for autographs. There were seven or eight vast rooms taken over by the convention that used to house upscale "anchor" stores, but now some of them featured more celebrities and others were for vendors of every stripe, including tattoo artists, ice cream and fudge makers, T-shirt and costume vendors, book and video marketers -- almost anything one could imagine.

I had attended at least a dozen movie conventions in various cities where Derrick and I were both guests, and at most of them I had noticed the same young girl who was with him now and had wondered why he never introduced her. She didn't seem to be of much assistance to him. She never sat beside him at his tables -- instead she always sat cross-legged on the floor against the black drapes at the back of his booth and under his banner. Was she one of his groupies? One of his relatives? Or what? He never seemed to acknowledge her. Whatever was going on between the two of them, it was quite strange and I couldn't figure it out. She always wore tight jeans and tight sweaters and had a lithe, athletic, well-formed figure. At this point Derrick was in his forties and she looked to be about nineteen. At previous conventions I had noticed that she seemed to bear a resemblance to him, a resemblance I thought might have been

stronger but for the fact that he had had his nose done. A common enough showbiz thing and not usually acknowledged

35

by those who invested in it. But back when I was contemplating casting him in one of my films, I had seen an article that talked about his time as a soldier in Vietnam, with an accompanying photo from when his nose protruded more and had a hook in it. The more I thought about it, the more I wondered if the girl with the unaltered nose was related to him in some way, but I never would have asked him about it since it seemed he wasn't anxious to let me know.

I'm well aware that for the sake of tactfulness these kinds of speculations are not usually openly talked about, but in a murder investigation nothing is sacred. Out of necessity, all sorts of things must come to light even if people have been trying to hide them.

Fridays are always the slow days at these events, but the hours are long, usually from five to ten PM, with "early birds" who have paid top price allowed to enter at 4:30. I got my booth set up with twenty minutes to spare before the arrival of the early birds, then freshened myself up in the men's room and lazed my way over to Derrick's lair. These events were always decidedly informal, so I was in jeans and a short-sleeved shirt and he was wearing a black skin-tight T-shirt, black jeans, black laced-up boots and a black watch cap with his black ponytail dangling out of it. He beard and mustache were -- what else -- thick and black. Neither of us spoke at first. His booth had five beautifully executed busts of iconic movie actors on prominent display, priced steeply at three thousand dollars apiece: Bela Lugosi, Peter Cushing, Ingrid Pitt, Duane Jones and Christopher Lee. I walked back and forth gazing at his sculptures to let him see how much I admired them. He had sculpted them himself and they showed a depth of talent that was missing from his acting. In his twisted path through the movie biz, he had missed his true calling. As a young man freshly graduated from the Art Institute of Pittsburgh, he had charged into Hollywood thinking he'd quickly find fame as a set design and makeup effects wizard. When lightning didn't strike, he started volunteering to perform dangerous stunts on low-budget productions in the hopes of getting licensed by the Stuntmen's Association. And when that ambition failed to materialize over the next few years, he morphed himself into a "Hair Design Artist" and by that unusual route he got himself "discovered" and molded into an action star by Lance Goldman.

I found myself pondering one of his sculptures that had stood out in my mind but was now missing -- a bust of Boris Karloff as Frankenstein -- which could mean either that it was sold or that the disturbingly weird story I had heard about it was actually true. At the premiere of the movie I had cast him in, I was told by his female co-star in one of Goldman International's *Scarifier* sequels that the bust originally was of Derrick's father, but he had formed the face of Frankenstein on top of it, then smashed it to bits with a baseball bat. If true, that anecdote might have all sorts of Freudian ramifications, but how was I to ascertain that?

I put on a friendly smile and said, "Why don't we abscond somewhere after the show closes and down a couple of drinks? I can tell you some interesting things about the murder investigation."

He said, "Well, I realize you wormed your way in on it. You and your buddy Vito. Not to mention your pretty daughter."

"Keep your hands off her," I said as though it were a joke, except I meant it.

Derrick chuckled with a touch of slyness that I did not like. He didn't shake my hand, nor did he introduce me to the girl who was still sitting cross-legged on the floor under his banner, even though I cast a long glance at her. She seemed not to be paying any attention to either of us.

"Sure, we'll get together for a drink," he said. "I'd like that."

I figured he was probably being more receptive than usual because he wanted to pick my brain as much as I wanted to pick his.

I went back to my booth to greet the onslaught of the early birds. When it erupted, even though Friday would be the slowest day I had lines at my table almost the entire time, and I noticed that Hubbara did, too, but his lines were three times longer than mine. I took in over two thousand dollars selling stills and posters from my movies plus tie-ins like articulated toys of some of the main characters. My price was twenty dollars per autographed item whether the fan already owned it or bought it from me at my booth.

Derrick Hubbara was selling the kinds of souvenirs and mementoes that I was, in addition to his steeply priced sculptures, but his lines were much longer than mine because he was a star who was very current and very big at the moment. I had once heard him bragging that he always took in as much as a hundred thousand bucks at every convention and it was all in cash. He said he would come home and toss the bundles into a safe in his bedroom without even doing a count. I always figured that most convention guests never reported this kind of income or at least not all of it, on their tax filings. (In case you're wondering whether or not I do, I'm not going to tell you.)

There is nothing quite like the gleeful rush into these events of folks who are borderline giddy about the opportunity to mingle with hundreds of like-minded enthusiasts. Horror fans by and large, even the ones sporting gory-looking tattoos and carrying fake knives, swords or machetes, were some of the happiest and friendliest people one could ever meet up with. I had done probably several hundred of these conventions over the past twenty years and had never seen a fight break out. My hard-core fans were overjoyed to see me. shake my hand, and get an autograph or a photo taken with me. Sometimes they flattered me, calling me a genius or a living legend or whatever, and I usually said, "Hey, I put my pants on one leg at a time like everybody else." Some of the pretty young women would shake when they stood close to me or pressed against me as our picture was being taken, as if they wanted a photo that made us look like we were boyfriend and girlfriend. But I never came on to them the way Hubbara would, especially with the cute ones, even when his enigmatic feminine companion was watching him.

At about a quarter till ten, a loudspeaker announcement told all of us it was nearly closing time and we should prepare to close up and come back for more fun tomorrow, ten AM for regular pass holders and 9:30 for early birds. I put lightweight black plastic sheets over my tables and looked toward Derrick's booth to see if he was ready to go for drinks, but his tables were already covered and he wasn't around, so I left, thinking I'd probably run into him. I did run into him out in the hall, and he was with Miss Whatever Her Name Was. They both looked uncomfortable and I thought they may have been arguing.

He said, "Can I have a rain check on the drinks, Dave? Something has come up."

"Okay," I said. "Maybe tomorrow will be better because the celebrity rooms close at seven."

I was trying to sound nonchalant while still keeping alive the possibility of furtively milking him for any information he might have withheld from the police. At least he hadn't flatly turned me down. Hope beats eternal in the human breast.

In terms of dealing with fans and attendees, Saturday was like Friday, except a lot more of it. At two o'clock I was scheduled to do a Q&A on *How to Write a Dynamic Horror Script*, so I covered my tables and headed to one of the panel rooms. Back when I was new to the movie business and its

39

attendant need for self-promotion I tended to freeze up in front of large audiences even though I was fine when pitching small groups of two to four. But over the years I had gotten a lot better and had lost the jitters. This time the room was packed, and the aspiring writers and filmmakers were highly appreciative and enthusiastic. They intently absorbed the fine points of plotting and conceptualizing and laughed at my lighthearted jokes. One of my staples was to tell them that making movies was a grueling process so they had to exercise regularly and stay in good shape to maintain the stamina. Then I would say, "It helps a lot if you have good genes. Mine are Wranglers." It might have been a silly pun, but it still got a laugh.

And as my time was up Derrick Hubbara was coming down the aisle, so the outbreak of applause was partly for me and partly for him as he "ascended" onto the dais with a self-satisfied smirk on his face, and I knew he was there to conduct his own scheduled Q&A, so I decided to stick around for part of it.

He began by casting a look in my direction that did not radiate friendliness. Then he said, "Some *guy* cast me in one of his movies and wouldn't let me make full use of my talents, which was like cutting off his nose to spite his face as far as his movie was concerned. I know all of you aren't that stupid! A lot of you are aware that I'm not just a damn good actor, I'm also a stunt man, a Black Belt in judo and Karate, a certified expert with knives, guns, swords and slingshots and crossbows and anything else you can name, even a bull whip, like that old-time movie cowboy, Lash LaRue. I mean, I can snake that whip around a guy's neck and strangle him to death. Yet this *guy* stopped me from doing something that would've given him a fabulous moment in his own movie."

Each time he said "this *guy*" he laid into it heavily and he and I both knew he was referring to me. His ego was such that he wanted to insult me in public without taking the full plunge by dropping my name. Totally incensed, I just stood there staring at him while he went on with his diatribe.

"All I wanted to do was fire a blank without telling these other two actors I was gonna do it when the camera was rolling for their reaction shots. We would've gotten some great stunned and totally unrehearsed looks on their faces in close-up! But that's when this *guy* called a halt to the scene and told me I couldn't fire a gun. He said it wasn't allowed by the Screen Actors Guild. Now how *stupid* is that? Blanks are fired all the time in movies, and I should know because I'm an expert on every weapon under the sun-- right? But he cut off his own nose to spite his face and put the kibosh on what would absolutely have been a great two-shot."

This got boos and hisses from his fans, but they were meant for me, not him, because they were totally enamored of their famous action hero, who was failing to realize why guns shouldn't be fired anytime he wished to do so. By Screen Actors Guild rules, actors must be warned every time blanks are to be fired because not just the actors but everybody on set needs to be given a chance to use ear plugs to cut down on the danger of concussion damaging their eardrums. Not only that, but there's a little thing called "acting ability" that will guarantee perfectly fine reaction shots without ear-drum damage. But Hubbara was bent on ripping into "this *guy*" who had thwarted an idea of his that was pure genius or at least it was what his addled ego persisted in believing.

I went back to my booth, stifling my urge to butt heads with him because of my need to get something out of him that might aid our investigation. I didn't want to disappoint Vito and Joy and I hoped they were having better luck in Los Angeles.

CHAPTER 7

My dad, writer and movie director David Cristi, asked me to write certain chapters of this book, specifically the ones which pertain to my part in the story during times when he was otherwise engaged. I'm his daughter, Joy Cristi, which you already know unless you skipped over some of the opening chapters. My full-time job for the past several years has been working with private investigator Vito Martinelli at his firm, Victor Martin Associates, which is sort of a misnomer and an in-joke, which you also are aware of, and I hope it gave you a chuckle. I appreciate Vito's sense of humor partly because I'm as flippant and sassy as he is. It's one of my endearing qualities, according to my father, except he may be one of the few people who are genuinely endeared by it.

I used to be Joy Bettinger, but got divorced four years ago and took my birth name back. I feel more comfortable in it. Also more independent, which I believe I was meant to be, until I got hooked up with a domineering husband who carried a lot of hidden baggage. I don't harbor a grudge against Michael. But good riddance. It took me far too long to recognize that he was smothering me, and now I relish my freedom all the more.

In writing parts of this book, which is largely by and about my own father, I'm reminded of Samuel Clemens's daughter Susy, who as a little girl began to write a charming biography of him from a child's perspective. Of course I'm not a little girl anymore, but I probably share with Susy some of the emotions resulting from having a famous father. She was bright, perceptive and introspective beyond her years, but unfortunately she didn't live long. At age twenty-four, a few years younger than I am now, she was struck down by spinal meningitis and Sam and his wife Livy were notified by telegram while they were aboard a ship crossing the Atlantic Ocean and could not rush home to be with her. Then a second telegram came, notifying them that, thank God, Susy was on her way to recovery. But this was soon followed by a third telegram telling them that Susy had died, and Samuel Clemens wrote, "It is one of the wonders of human nature that a man can take a blow like that, all unprepared, and still live."

I know my father loves me every bit as much as Mark Twain loved Susy. And he worries that by working with Vito something terrible might happen to me. But he's the one who taught me to be daring and to embrace life. And not only that, but to embrace it fully and dare to pursue your dreams, you have to have a bit of defiance in you. Because in the movie business and in life in general, there are always people who want to pull you down in order to climb over you. The "crabs in a barrel" syndrome.

I think I got my appetite for adventure when my dad introduced me to Tom Sawyer and Huckleberry Finn when I was in grade school. I wanted to travel down a river on a raft just like they did. I was always a tomboy because they seemed to have more fun. And what's more they were allowed to.

I worry about my father as much or more than he worries about me, and I think he knows

it. No matter what happens, we look out for each other. He loves his wife, my stepmother Diane, very much, and so do I. I stay in touch with my birth mother, Danielle Stanwix, who's an actress working in Los Angeles and sometimes in New York, but I have more in common with Diane. I think that sometimes the movie actress Danielle Stanwix, who is not quite a star but yearns to be, buys far too much into Hollywood glitz, glamour and phoniness. My dad is more down to earth. And so am I. Because of who he is, I've met lots of people in the biz and I've never been overly impressed with them.

As a matter of fact, Vito Martinelli is a lot like my dad in that he does not suffer fools gladly. Until he and I flew to Los Angeles, I had never met Victoria Goldman, but I probably would have if Dad's *Dealey Plaza* mini-series hadn't gotten scuttled for such dire reasons. Things would certainly have been much different. I would probably have met her on some kind of far more pleasant occasion, for instance, if she would've come to Pittsburgh during casting or pre-production or on location once shooting started. But as it turned out, a limo was waiting for us at LAX, which took us directly to Victoria's office at Lance International Pictures.

She wasn't wearing her grief on her sleeve; in other words, she had herself under control no matter how many tears she might have shed in private. I had already seen photos of her as a result of my prior research. She was fifty-two years old, eleven years younger than her husband had been when he was killed, and to me she looked no older than forty, and her youthfulness did not appear to have been augmented by surgery although I doubted that ash blonde without any trace of gray in it was her natural color. Wikipedia had given me her statistics: Five, six; 135; 37-34-36. She was a former actress, now a CEO and before that a head. of acquisitions, which meant she had given her approval to the making of a movie based on my father's most important and ambitious novel, so I tended to think well of her right off the bat.

Instead of sitting behind her imposing mahogany desk, she beckoned me and Vito to a maroon leather couch and sat opposite us in a gray leather armchair and instead of engaging in chit-chat the executive side of her took over and she said, "I don't believe in wasting my mine or yours. I understand how quickly cases go cold, and if I have anything to do with it that is not going to happen. I asked you to be ready to go to work when you got here, and I meant it.""No problem. We're on the same page with that," Vito said. "Joy and I are prepared to be off and running."

I backed him up by bending toward the case that held my laptop, picking it up and opening it.

Victoria said, "I would hope so because one of the persons on my list is due to arrive here shortly."

Vito didn't act surprised so I didn't either as I set my laptop on a coffee table and booted it up. Meantime there was a tentative rap on the office door which swung open to reveal a perfectly coiffed and stylishly attired brunette who didn't lack for poise and presence any more than Victoria did, though she was about ten years younger, which I knew from my research, so I called her up on my laptop. There was a photo gallery picturing her at various ages and in an array of character costumes, but today she was wearing elegant designer jeans and a sleek, silvery, short-sleeved blouse with delicate silver earrings and a silver necklace.

Victoria arose and said, "Thank you for coming, Alicia. You may have my chair. I have other business to attend to. Meet Detective Martinelli and his associate, Joy Cristi. They're here to interview you."

"Pleased to meet you," Alicia said. "I'm aware of some of your previous murder cases. I must admit I'm impressed."

"So are we," Vito said as Victoria exited and shut the door. "We have your resume and we're glad you're here."

"Well, it's my duty and I want to help," said Alicia. "My dispute with Lance Goldman was resolved to my satisfaction and his, so I had no reason to wish him dead. My hope is that I can convince you to look elsewhere."

"So you didn't hold a grudge against him?" Vito asked in spite of her protestation.

"He didn't try to blackball me," Alicia said with a self-amused smile. "Currently I have a supporting role in a TV series called *Baker's Run.*"

"I've seen it," I said, glancing up from my laptop. "You're very good in it."

She said, "Thank you, Joy." And her smile brightened.

I wasn't above using a bit of flattery, especially when it was sincere and not totally sneaky. I also knew that Vito was disposed to believe I had a way of putting other women at ease and causing them to open up.

Alicia Simmons wasn't one of the two women who had filed sexual harassment claims against Lance Goldman. Her dispute wasn't of that nature, and we knew it from my research.

Nevertheless we needed to get her take on it, so Vito asked, "Do you mind telling us what your beef with Lance International Pictures was all about and how it worked out for you? We'd like the true scoop for our report. We don't really suspect you of anything. We're just doing due diligence at this point, the same as we would do for any other investigation."

"No doubt in my mind about that," said Alicia. "I've done a few cop shows so I'm a bit savvy, not an expert by any means, but probably hipper than the average TV addict."

"You research your roles?" Vito asked.

"It gives me an edge, or at least I like to think so."

"Yep, I can see that," said Vito. "So what can you tell us about your dealings with Lance?"

"I really had nothing specifically against him. I didn't file against him personally, just his company."

"What about his wife? She wasn't too happy with you either, was she?"

"I wouldn't think so. But she signed the inadequate checks that were sent to me and probably knew the statements were inaccurate. Everybody who's been in our business very long knows about something called creative accounting. It's a

46

euphemism for cheating, skimming or scamming. Whoever touches the money first -- and it's usually the studios or the producers -- keeps as much of it as possible instead of paying it out fairly. Points off of the back end are used to grease deals, but production and marketing costs are always inflated or falsely attributed, so no movie ever shows a profit on paper. I was too naive to know that in the beginning but when I got wiser, I didn't stand still for it. Luckily my father was just as incensed as I was, and he's a wealthy and brilliant entertainment attorney who knows how to do a thorough audit. Lance Goldman didn't know it, and he found out the hard way."

"So your father got you a substantial settlement?" Vito said.

"Damn right he did," said Alicia. "I had no reason to kill Lance Goldman."

Vito tuned to me and said, "Anything you'd like to ask, Joy?"

One of the reasons I liked working for Vito Martinelli was that he never treated me like a laptop flunky. He always made it clear that I was an integral part of his investigative team so the folks we had to deal with would be inclined to respect me. When I first started with him, with a goal of earning my own PI license, I was a bit overwrought about my ability to please him, but by now it was sort of a given between us that I had his back and he had mine.

I said to Alicia, "If you had to guess at a potential suspect or a motive, who or what would most readily come to mind, in your view?"

She mulled it over, then said, "Well, I could come up with a string of people who had reason to be unhappy with Lance or Victoria personally. But I can't picture any of them being devious enough or obsessed enough to carry out a long-distance murder plot. I hope you find out who did it, but I'd be terribly upset if it turns out to be anybody I know, and I refuse to believe it will turn out that way."

CHAPTER 8

I was still fuming over the way Derrick Hubbara had put me down by repeatedly calling me *this guy* instead of insulting me by name. Obviously he got off by doing it so slyly while seeking solace for his bruised ego from a room full of his fans. Maybe he thought he would be safe from a libel suit by treating me so anonymously. Maybe he had wanted to provoke a fist fight that he would surely win. I was in good shape for my age, but he was almost thirty years younger and a lot stronger. And he was right about one thing: he was an expert in all kinds of martial arts. I was pigeonholed as a *gore master*, an epithet I hated for selling me short, but by the same token I had him pigeonholed as a Hollywood *careerist*, a groper after fame and money and not a true artist and certainly not an intellectual. He had made it through a lucky hookup with Lance Goldman who had recognized that his charisma and his physique would resound on the silver screen, making the teeny-boppers swoon. Lance had created a monster. Not a rare phenomenon in show business. Or politics for that matter. We already had endured Reagan and Schwarzenegger and I feared that worse was yet to come. But for the moment I had to pretend I was unfazed by Hubbara's public put-down of me, so I approached him after show hours on Saturday as he was heading toward the hotel bar and was not accompanied by the incognito young woman I didn't know anything about.

I said, "I was hoping to run into you, Derrick."

He tensed up as if ready to raise his fists. But I put on a friendly smile and said, "I'm up for a drink or two. Want to find a corner where we can sit and talk?"

"About what?" he said warily.

"As you know, my daughter and I work closely with Vito Martinelli and we're looking into Lance Goldman's murder at his wife's behest. You might be interested in hearing some of what we've found out so far."

I knew that careerists, mad strivers like him, were transactional creatures, therefore I had chosen to imply that he had something to gain from me, rather than the other way around.

"Sure, let's talk," he said with a showbiz smile, taking the bait.

But the bar and all the tables and chairs were full so we stopped in our tracks. I didn't want to suggest going to some other place. I might lose him if I did that. He might want to rejoin his enigmatic lady friend.

Luckily, two of his fans spotted us having no place to sit and immediately got up and offered us their booth. They were both bearded and sported man buns and in so in awe of the great Derrick Hubbara that they hiked their pants up to show him that they had images of him from one of his *Scarifier* spinoffs tattooed on their calves. "We don't want to take your seats," I said to them.

One of them said, "We'd be honored if you did, Mr. Cristi. Don't worry, we'll muscle in on our friends up there at the bar. They'll gladly make room once we tell them it's for you. We're all huge fans."

The other fellow said, "You two guys are living legends, man!"

And his buddy said, "Amen!" And they bumped fists.

I smiled and said, "I put my pants on one leg at a time like everybody else."

They chortled as they sheepishly backed away and headed toward their pals.

Derrick and I sat down, knowing that if any other fans wanted to talk to us or take selfies we'd have to demur by telling them we were talking business. A waitress immediately came over and we ordered bottles of Blue Moon. It seemed that we were being treated with even more deference than usual by our fans and by the hotel staff, and I thought it might be because it was so widely known that a noted movie producer had been murdered on his way to meet with us not far from here.

Derrick said, "Why did you tell those fan boys you put your pants on one leg at a time. We're gods to them. You should let them keep thinking that way."

"Maybe you're right," I conceded. But I didn't mean it. I was trying to find common ground with him for the time being. Otherwise I would've told him it was fine with me if they liked my work, but I didn't want to be on anybody's pedestal.

Just then a teenybopper rushed toward us, looking angry.

Derrick jerked toward her, looking startled.

She spat, "I knew I'd find you *here* after I looked all over for you, Daddy *Dear!*"

She laid on that last word as sarcastically as he had called me *this guy*. I realized she was

his daughter , although I hadn't recognized her at first. Her looks and demeanor were quite changed from what they were four years ago when he had wanted me to cast her along with him in my movie and I had refused. Back then she was a cute grade-school kid and now she was a flippant adolescent in a TV series about kids fighting zombies. That was the image she still had to portray on television but it seemed she was rebelling against it off-screen. Her blonde hair was dyed pink and green; she wore big hoop earrings, a necklace with a pendant in the shape of a silver dragon, a low-cut red blouse

51

that almost made her nipples pop out, and shiny blue and silver and very clingy bellbottom pants. She seemed to be trying hard to present herself as a haughty, sophisticated young actress but was coming off mean and snotty.

"Is your *girlfriend* here?" she said as she jammed a cigarette between her waxy, overly lipsticked red lips.

"Shut up and sit down," Derrick told her, making room for her on his side of the booth. "And don't light that cigarette. You have to go outside to smoke."

"Stupid rules!" she scoffed broke the cigarette in two, and dropped it onto the tabletop, leaking shreds of tobacco.

"Nice to see you," Derrick said, sweeping the cigarette's remains onto the floor.

She sneered and demanded, "Where's Carla?"

"None of your business."

She shrugged, then looked at me and said, "I'm glad you didn't cast me. I'm doing bigger and better *things* now."

I said, "I'm really happy for you."

She said, "I'll bet." Then she jerked her head toward the bar and suddenly twisted her lithe young body out of our booth, saying, "Oh! There's Billy! I have to talk to him!"

Watching her go, Derrick said, "I see who she means. Bill Snyder, that heavy-metal jerk who makes horror movies now."

She didn't get stopped by any of the fans as she sashayed across the floor, which would certainly have happened if she had been recognized as the actress, Jenny Huber. But she had overdone herself too much.

"Well, at least she's getting famous and seems to enjoy it," I said.

"I liked her better before," Derrick admitted. "You have a daughter, don't you? How do you get along with her?"

"Fine. Couldn't be better. But I probably worry about her too much because she works with Vito on murder cases sometimes. So do I."

"That's well known, Dave."

"Of course. And it's why I wanted to talk with you. Do you know anything more than I do about Lance Goldman's itinerary on the day he was kidnapped and killed?"

Derrick clouded up and said, "Hey, man, I thought you were going to clue *me* in on some things, so don't put it all on me, buddy boy."

Buddy boy immediately went into my anthology of terms I despised, along with *gore master* and *let's get in bed on this*. I stifled a groan and said, "I think it wouldn't hurt if we both *share* information. Clue each other in, in other words."

"Okay. You first," he shot back at me.

"Anything I tell you must be kept in strict confidence," I warned him. "If some of it gets out it will only help the murderers, either right now or whenever the case comes to trial."

He nodded his assent, then decided to say something in his usual arrogant way. "You want me to sign an NDA, for Chrissake?"

I ignored that comment and sucked in a deep breath, then gave him a brief summation of what Vito and I had learned from Sheriff Boyce. I was trying not to reveal anything that might hurt the case, yet I felt I had to give him something tangible so he'd perhaps trust me a bit more. So I did reveal that the murder weapon was "possibly" a Luger -- couching the revelation in the word "possible," although we knew that's what it was for certain. I was surprised that he blinked as I said it.

"You look startled," I ventured.

"Just that I'd expect it to be a Glock. All the gangbangers have them these days."

"You think Lance's murder is the work of gangbangers?"

"Maybe. Why not?"

"Well, if the motive was a carjacking, that limo would've been driven right to Mexico, or to a chop shop, not torched in a warehouse. I think they believed it wouldn't even be found for several days. And they wanted all the evidence to go up in flames, including the murder weapon."

Derrick's daughter came back to the booth just then, interrupting my effort to pump him. And she had in tow a wiry little fellow who couldn't have been much taller than five foot four.

"Daddy, meet my new boyfriend," she said. "Giorgio this is my dad, the great Blaze Stewart. At least that's who he plays in the movies. But he's really Derrick Hubbara, just like I'm Jennifer Hubbara, not Jenny Huber."

Derrick nodded and looked pissed. He glowered at little Giorgio, who had a thick crop of black, bushy hair and perfectly sculpted sideburns the length of his jaws, with no mustache or beard. He was wearing jeans, sneakers and a plain black T-shirt, so I saw that his arms were like pipestems. All together, he was the antithesis of Derrick Hubbara alias Blaze Stewart, and I wondered if that was why his daughter was smirking at him.

Jenny didn't bother introducing me to Giorgio. Instead, she said, "See you later, Daddio!" And tugged Giorgio by his hand, leading him to the bar.

"Let's get the hell outta here," Derrick said. "I'm sick of this joint. I don't wanna talk anymore."

He got up and out of the booth so quickly that he left me sitting there as he stormed out.

At least I had learned the name of his enigmatic female friend, the one who lurked at his booth without getting introduced to me or anyone else that I knew of. Jenny had spoken her name, Carla, with contempt or outright hatred. Derrick was a compulsive womanizer and Jenny was obviously a rebellious teenager who might reject her father's conquests out of jealousy or fear of abandonment.

I was glad that I wasn't having an affair before I divorced Danielle, my first wife. I had feared I would lose Joy, and I knew how lucky I was that in the end that didn't happen, in spite of some emotional damage to both of us along the way.

CHAPTER 9

On Friday, after our ride in from LAX, Vito and I only had time enough for one interview, the one with actress Alicia Simmons. But on Saturday morning we got up bright and early at our hotel, the Beverly Hilton, took a cab to Victoria's office. We had told her before leaving on Friday that we would like to schedule the two women who had filed sexual harassment charges as the first two interviews come Saturday morning. My research had shown that both of the accusers had filed similar claims and were each other's prime witnesses. This smacked of collusion in our opinion. Eight years ago when they filed against Lance, their acting careers were not scintillating, they were rumored to be willing playthings on various casting couches, and they both ended up being paid huge amounts of money to sign NDA'S and go away permanently. Yet Victoria had easily succeeded in getting them to come in, with a minimum of cajoling, and this suggested that they were still out for scraps of notoriety or for one more little story they could sell to the tabloid newspapers or TV shows.

In spite of all that, Vito and I didn't give them short shrift. We asked each of them in turn enough questions and harvested enough answers to satisfy ourselves that their stories were carbon copies of each other, just as they had been eight years ago. Plus neither of them seemed bright enough to pull off the kind of kidnapping and murder plot we were dealing with. We weren't going to forget about them, but for now they were on the back burner.

By eleven AM, as the day's second interviewee left Victoria's office, Vito and I shrugged at one another and I whispered, "Waste of time."

"Not really," he said. "Eliminating suspects is as much progress as nailing them. Also a vital part of the job."

"Yeah, I know," I said grumpily.

"Seriously," he said, "do you see any reason to bring either of them back?"

"Nope."

Victoria's secretary stepped in and said, "The next one isn't due for fifteen more minutes. Would you like coffee, juice or water?"

"Water, please," I said, and Vito asked for apple juice.

I called up my notes on our next person of interest. Jose Della Cruz was a prop master who had been beaten up on a movie set by -- guess who? -- none other than Derrick Hubbara. It was a startling fact that we did not know when we were back in Pittsburgh, and Victoria hadn't clued us to it till she greeted us this morning. For some reason Hubbara's nasty involvement had been withheld from her brief notes on the five persons she had listed of potential suspects. She had merely stated that Mr. Della Cruz "had been assaulted by an actor and had sued Lance International Pictures for payment of his medical bills, loss of income and severe, incapacitating emotional damage."

When Veronica's secretary ushered Della Cruz to us, we saw that he had a limp and a sagging right shoulder. He was in his early forties, according to his short bio on *iMDB*, but he moved like a much older man with a degenerative bone disease to boot. He had a dark-complexioned face, deep-set black eyes that narrowed during bursts of pain, and not much gray in his wavy combed-back hair. He was wearing faded jeans and a Mickey Mouse T-shirt and carried a can that he hadn't used.

Sitting down with a repressed groan, he immediately started spewing his grievances. "That bastard Derrick Hubbara came up behind me and knocked me down with a judo chop. I wasn't like I am now -- five years ago I was a pretty strong guy. But he kicked me over and over, then stomped on my chest. Not just once -- I don't really know how many times. I woke up in the hospital. And I didn't get in a single punch!"

"What did he say to you while it was happening?" Vito asked. "Did he yell anything at you?"

"No, he was too busy beating on me. But he told the cops I had left a dumdum in his prop pistol. You know what a dumdum is?"

Vito and I both knew but we acted as though we didn't, just to hear it from him.

"A fake bullet," he explained. "Not the whole bullet, just the front, the part that kills, made out of painted wood. See? If you film a revolver head-on and there's nothing showing in the cylinder, people are gonna know it's not ready to shoot, so you need something in there for the audience to buy that it's loaded. But when you're gonna fire a blank you have to remove all the dumdums or else they'll come blasting out of there just like the head of a live round."

"I think that's what killed Brandon Lee," Vito said.

"Damn right it did," said Mr. Della Cruz. "Somebody forgot to extract the dumdum, maybe even left it in there on purpose like some of the tabloids said, and when that other actor, playing the bad guy, fired the weapon at Brandon Lee -- directly at him instead of to the side, for safety, because the camera won't actually know the difference if it's done right -- the dumdum tore into Brandon's guts and he bled to death."

"I remember reading about it," Joy said. "I was a fan of those martial arts movies when I was a little girl."

"I don't watch them," Della Cruz said. "I never used to neither, even when I helped make them. I *never* liked them personally, but they paid good. Now I can't work no more. No way did I ever leave a dumdum in a revolver when we were done taking frontal shots and had to fire a blanks in the next setup. Every prop master in the business will never forget what happened to Brandon Lee -- and Jon Hexum too."

"Hexum?" Vito said.

"Jon Eric Hexum. A real up-and-coming star. His career was taking off big. Till he put a gun to his temple, just clowning around with a prop, he must've thought, but there was a blank in the chamber and it blasted pieces of his skull into his head. He was on life support till they found out he was brain dead, then the machines were turned off."

Vito nodded toward me so I could ask a question if I had one.

I said, "Please be honest with me, Mr. Della Cruz. Did you hold a grudge against Lance Goldman because of what his big star did to you?"

He stiffened, grimacing with pain and reddening with anger. "No fuckin' way! But

Hubbara is another story. If someone doused *him* with gasoline, I'd gladly toss a lit match. But Goldman and his wife, they treated me as good as they could. They didn't even my claim tooth and nail. They treated my lawyer like a decent person, a gentleman doin' his job. And yessir! They paid up right away. Otherwise, I'd be in a nursing home or living in a cardboard box under a bridge."

Vito said, "That will be all for today, Mr. Della Cruz. May we count on you if we need to ask follow-up questions? Something else might come up as our investigation proceeds."

"You bet," he said. "I got nothing against Lance Goldman and I want his killer to be caught. And his limousine driver didn't need to be die that way either. It's a cruel son of a bitch who would do a thing like that."

After he left, Vito turned to me and said, "Let's have a little talk with Victoria on our way out of here. But pack up your laptop so she doesn't feel threatened. She needs to tell us why she didn't level with us about Derrick Hubbara."

Victoria's secretary buzzed her, and she agreed to have us ushered into a plush conference room where she had apparently been working while allowing us to use her own office for our interviews. She was sitting in a big red upholstered leather chair with a laptop, a phone and an assortment of notepads and writing utensils spread out before her., and she was wearing a simple pink blouse and designer jeans. Vito and I sat close to her in two of the matching chairs around the polished eight-foot conference table with seating for eight.

Getting right down to the matter at hand, Vito said, "I'm curious as to why you let me and Joy be blindsided by Jose Della Cruz instead of cluing us in about Derrick Hubbara's assault on him."

She didn't balk at being challenged. Matter-of-factly maintaining her composure, she said, "I wanted to see if Joy would somehow dig it up without any help from me. We had paid off all the right people to keep the story buried back then, and I was hoping it had stayed that way, or else our money wouldn't have been well spent."

"In other words," Vito said, "you and your husband wanted to protect your biggest in-house star from facing a huge scandal or a possible prison sentence."

"Guilty as charged," Victoria answered without apologizing. "You should just take it in stride since I'm paying your tab."

"What do you say to that, Joy?" Vito asked.

"It rankles a bit," I answered for his benefit as well as Victoria's, "but I can understand it as a necessary business decision on behalf of the company and its shareholders."

"Smart girl," said Victoria. "I'm glad to have you here. You're a pragmatist, not a wimp."

"However," I said, "my main question has to be whether or not Derrick Hubbara's motive for his attack on Mr. Della Cruz was the complete truth or a made up story? And if it wasn't true, did he have help concocting it?"

"Certainly not," Victoria said, slightly incensed. "We only had Derrick's word for it, because Della Cruz didn't offer a counter story. He acted like he was anxious to put the incident behind him. He took the money and ran."

"But he doesn't sound like a liar," I ventured. "He comes off like a simple hardworking man, not a money grubber. Unless he had me and Vito both fooled."

"Well, wait a minute, Joy," Vito chided me. "Derrick was with your father at Pittsburgh

International, waiting for Lance when the kidnapping and murder went down. That's why we know he's in the clear unless he hired someone. But why would he? What's his motive? He's all about himself and his career. Lance International Pictures put him on top."

"Damn right we did," Victoria said with utter determination. "This company is going to thrive. I'm perfectly capable of running it just as well as my husband did. And maybe better. We already had a shareholder meeting and nobody rose up against me. They wouldn't dare. They know where their bread is buttered just as well as Derrick does."

"That I can believe," Vito told her. "Ready to go, Joy?'

I said that I was, and we took our leave, wanting to think we were still in Victoria's good graces.

"At least she didn't fire us," I said after we stepped onto the elevator.

"For now," said Vito. "But are you thinking what I'm thinking?"

"We have to clear her as a suspect," I answered. "It seems she's gained more than anyone else from her husband's demise."

We got off the elevator, exited the building and started looking around for the taxi we had phoned ahead for. Not there yet.

Vito said, "I hate to open up a can of worms but..."

"But what?" I prodded.

"There's little doubt that someone hated Lance Goldman enough to want him dead and went to great lengths to make it happen. And we've been thinking that since he's a bigwig out here, but a fairly recent development, the killer's grudge has to be a recent thing. But what if it isn't? What if someone from way back in his life had a reason to hate him but the hatred didn't become virulent till Lance acquired all the trappings of wealth and fame?"

"Wow! That does open a whole new can of worms," I said. "An old, deeply entrenched

motive instead of a new one. But..." My voice trailed off as I hesitated.

"But what?" Vito asked.

"We'd be doing the right thing by delving a whole lot more into Lance's early days. But I'm thinking we need to look more deeply into the limo driver too. We've been operating on the theory that Lance was the target and the driver was collateral damage, but what if it was the other way around?"

"Holy shit, Joy! Why didn't *I* think of that? I guess that's why I pay you the big bucks."

"Yeah, right," I chided, because he paid me pretty well but not big. But after all I didn't have my PI license yet and he could've hired someone with more experience.

"I think that's our cab," he said. "Yep. He's pulling over."

We hurried to the curb, the cabbie nodded at us. As we settled in and the cab eased into traffic, Vito said, "I'm glad we have such an early flight out of here. The case keeps expanding the longer we stay. However, one thing I'd like to do is get some Mexican food before we leave. Are you up for it?"

"Always up for that. L.A. has the best," I answered. "I'd hate it if we passed up the chance."

"After we eat," Vito said, "I'm going to stay in my room so I can phone Sheriff Boyce and report on our results so far out here. I'll let him know there's no reason for us not to head back to Pittsburgh and ask him if anything's shaking down in his area, in case he wants us there."

CHAPTER 10

Vito and I got up at six AM, figuring to have a leisurely continental breakfast, then head to LAX. As soon as we got to a table he told me that Sheriff Boyce was well satisfied with the way we were handling things and there were no new developments that would dictate we should head to Washington, Pennsylvania once we got back.

By seven we were sipping coffee when his cell phone buzzed. I could tell it was Victoria that he was talking to but couldn't catch the gist of the conversation. I waited for the call to end, hoping it wasn't some kind of bad news about my father even though I couldn't imagine what the bad news could be.

When Vito put his phone back in his pocket, he said, "I guess we're going to have more chances at great Mexican food. That was Victoria. We've got to cancel our flight."

I didn't dare to ask why. I just looked at the dour look on his face.

"Two more murders and another arson," he said. "A Lance International dialogue coach and what seems to have been an innocent person in the wrong place at the wrong time."

I was glad it wasn't about my father, but at the same time I was shocked because what Vito was telling me was we now had two more murders and another arson closely replicating what had already been done to Lance Goldman and his limousine driver. How coincidental. Except no good investigator believes in coincidences.

Vito told me, "Victoria pulled some strings with the Hollywood Division. This latest thing happened on their watch, and she says the captain and two or three of his sergeants have made a lot of money doing location security for Lance International. She pointed out the similarities to what we're already working on and stressed that I'm a sheriff's deputy. So you and I will be given the opportunity of being on the crime scene with her guy, Captain Charles Devereux. Victoria has cleared the way for us to utilize a studio vehicle for as long as we need to, so we don't have to monk around with a rental company. So let's hit the road, Jack -- I mean, Joy." He grinned at his intentional flub. Even under dire circumstances, he would try to crack jokes, and some of them were amusing not for their ingenuity but for their lack of it.

We hadn't checked out of our rooms yet, so our luggage could remain there while we caught a cab that took us to the studio, where in short order we hopped into a black Ford Bronco like the white one made famous by O.J. Simpson and got on the freeway. Vito made use of his lead foot and we soon took an off-ramp and arrived at the crime scene -- or scene(s) -- because it consisted of two major elements: a house that showed plenty of fire damage and, across the street from the house, a Chevy sedan with a dead man slumped behind the wheel. That's where the Hollywood Division captain was standing when we recognized him because of the gold leaf in the visor of his hat and went up to him.

Vito said, "Excuse me, Captain Devereux. Veronica Goldman spoke with you about us. I'm Vito Martinelli and this is Joy Cristi who's working with me on her husband's murder case."

"I know. In Pittsburgh," he responded. "I agree with her about the apparent similarities. I believe in cooperating with other law enforcement agencies, even the FBI. I never turn it into a pissing contest. If we can cooperate, maybe we can solve both cases."

I was pleased to hear him talk that way, and I knew that Vito would be too. The guy's entire bearing radiated "no nonsense." I guessed he was about forty. Very clean-cut, military fashion. Maybe he had some hair on the top of his head, under his hat, but his sideburns were shaved off high above his ears.

The corpse in the Chevy hadn't been carried away yet, and as we looked at it Captain Devereux said, "He took a round in his neck and another one in his face. See his cell phone on the seat there?"

Vito and I both came closer and peered into the vehicle, the interior sparsely lit by a nearby street lamp.

The captain said, "We figure he must've spotted the fire and pulled over to call 9-1-1. Hopefully the call got logged in and recorded, at least part of it, which we'll soon find out. We already know who the guy is because he had his wallet on him. He was a baggage handler at LAX and his shift ended at four AM and he was probably headed home. His driver's license gave us his name and address. Poor guy. He was trying to do the right thing."

"No good deed goes unpunished," said Vito.

"Not usually in this business," said Captain Devereux.

"What did you find in the house?" Vito asked him.

"Well, the fire inspector is still in there, but we already know gasoline was used. The guys with the hoses found two burnt and twisted two-gallon cans. Then they found the victim's body -- what's left of it. He must be the guy who lived here, but that might have to be confirmed through dental work or DNA because a lot of his face is gone. For right now, if we can assume as much, he's Darby Coltrane and he was on staff at Lance International Pictures. That's what prompted me to phone Victoria."

"Joy and I think this has at least a small chance of being related to Lance Goldman's murder," Vito said. "Wouldn't you think the same, Captain?"

"I can tell you this much. Coltrane wasn't outright killed, he was tortured first. Some of him is intact, thanks to the good Samaritan who died calling it in. When the firemen found him his right arm was almost totally charred and blistered, but his other one was partly folded under him, and when they put him in the body bag they saw all kinds of little puncture wounds and slashes on his biceps and forearms. Plus there seemed to have been a fairly large gasoline pour in his crotch area -- because that part of him was more charred than the rest. So I've gotta be thinking there's a sexual motive here. Maybe the autopsy will confirm or deny it."

Vito said, "It's a good thing whoever did this didn't succeed in burning the house to the ground. If they had succeeded we wouldn't have anything to speculate about."

I said, "We'd better get my dad out here so he can help us out, don't you think? Unless he's turned up something that warrants him staying in Pittsburgh a while longer."

"Hard to imagine anything more important than this," Vito said.

CHAPTER 11

On Sunday the Pittsburgh Horror Festival started winding down around three o'clock as the fans ran pretty much out of money and stopped spending. This was how most shows slowly petered out and this one was no exception. By four o'clock most of the out-of-town celebrities had been taken to the airport to make their flights and the locals, like me, generally lingered a while longer, packing up and saying our goodbyes.

After I got my stuff loaded into my car, I went back into the hotel to use the men's room one last time before driving home. But as I passed the bar a brassy voice called out, *"Hey,* Cristi, get your ass *in here!"*

I stopped in my tracks, scanned the semi-dark interior, and spotted Derrick Hubbara's ex-wife, Leona. Her raspy voice blared at me again, drunkenly. *"Hey,* buster, don't you wanna *interrogate me?* I know a lot of *showbiz shit,* Mr. Movie *Director!"*

I almost ignored her and kept walking. But then I thought better of it. Drunks were often very good snitches since their inhibitions were down and they were prone to indiscretion. Who would know Derrick Hubbara best -- warts and all -- other than a vindictive ex-wife? So I joined her at the bar, noting that there were empty seats on either side of her, probably because nobody else wanted any part of the unpleasantness.

She slurred, "So whaddaya like best, big shot? Real murders or fake ones?"

"If you call me a gore master, I'm leaving," I told her. "But if you control yourself I'll buy you a drink -- or several."

"I bet you don't even remember my name!"

"Sure I do. It's Leona."

"Bingo!" she said, laughing loudly and coarsely. "I admit I'm surprised! So you win the teddy bear -- the Derry Bear, the *Hew-bear-a!* Get it, buster?"

"Can we tone it down?" I said. "In fact, if you really have something important to tell me, let's get a booth."

There was a bartender in front of me right then, so I asked for a Blue Moon and Leona brassily proclaimed her desire for a "Quadruple shot of tequila." Then I paid and I carried both drinks to a booth in a corner because I thought she'd probably spill hers or drop the glass full, shattering it on the floor.

"Don't believe anything that crazy bitch tells you!" Derrick Hubbara's voice rang out suddenly, and I whirled around and saw him, half expecting him to come over and take a swing at me. But he didn't. He was with Carla and she was meekly tugging at his elbow -- and he surprised me by turning toward the dining room.

Leona called out, "That's right, *Derry Bear!* Get the hell outta here with your *floozy-doozy!"*

Then she turned to me and said, "That's his fucking *niece!* You *believe* that?"

I felt my eyes widen and my face tighten.

"Righto!" Leona brayed. "Carla is his fucking niece! I mean that literally. At least I think I do. He started parading naked around Jenny when she was only five years old! But I couldn't tell on him because he was my coke connection -- so he had me trapped and the son-of-a-bitch *knew* it, goddamn it! I finally had enough of his shit! But he got custody because I'm a drunk and a cokehead and his asshole buddies testified against *me!"*

"I've gotta go," I said, because my brain was reeling. I got up and left, taking my Blue Moon with me, craving a slug of it..

Leona called out in her screechy rasp, "Go on, Mister *Big Time!* You can't *stand* the truth -- just like Jack Nicholson said in that movie! Can't stand the truth -- *none* of you! How the fuck're the likes of *you* gonna solve Lance Goldman's *murder?"*

I didn't know if I should just ignore everything she was saying. Maybe I shouldn't believe a word of it. Or were there other, less damaging, interpretations? Maybe Derrick Hubbara didn't think anybody, including his own daughter, should be ashamed of nakedness. I recalled an assistant cameramen on one of my movies who liked to talk about his summer vacations at a nudist camp near Hershey, Pennsylvania, home of Hershey bars and Hershey Park where children could have innocent fun with their clothes on. Did primitive tribes worry about such things? Or did they all run shamelessly naked into their lakes or rivers, laughing a splashing and not erotically aroused in the slightest? Which was supposed to be the point of the nudist camps. Children and adults all went naked, and my assistant cameraman said it was a healthy attitude in contrast to the way that repressive religion had made us overly civilized people ashamed of our own bodies.

Case in point: When I used the men's room, temporarily setting my bottle of Blue Moon down next to a sink, I contemplated the partitions between the urinals. Were some men scared some guy at the nest urinal might glance over and compare penises?

After washing and drying my hands, I picked up my bottle of beer and sat on a chair in the hall where I was approached by an old friend, Gary Chelton, the movie artist and set designer who had made my banner for me without charging me for it. I knew he had also made Derrick Hubbara's banner. They often hobnobbed with one another at conventions and seemed to get off on being around each other. My opinion was that Gary seemed to think he was a colleague of Derrick's, but Derrick likely thought of him as just another fanboy.

"Hey, what're you doing drinking all by your lonesome?" Gary asked, chuckling as he walked up to me.

"I'm told that the girl who's always in Derrick's booth is his niece," was the first thing out of my mouth as I tried to keep my voice nonjudgmental.

Gary chuckled more sardonically this time, and said quite matter-of-factly, "Derrick's a narcissist, and the next thing to fucking yourself is fucking someone related to you." He didn't sound in the least censorious; instead he sounded accepting of it, as if it were a mere quirk.

"You don't much care?" I asked incredulously.

"Not really. To each his own. Edgar Allen Poe married his cousin. So did Jerry Lee Lewis. And Elvis was an obvious cradle robber. I try not to be too harsh on folks. We all have our shortcomings. Some of us even have skeletons in our closets. But I say live and let live. I don't think Derrick is as talented as he thinks he is, but don't tell him I said that. He's not a very good actor and he can't direct his way out of a paper bag. I buddied up to him to get hired onto that TV series he was a director on, *Tales from the Bone Orchard*. I thought it'd be a kick, man. But I was miserable the whole time, and so were most of my set builders. They were seasoned professionals and they saw right through him. We pegged him as a charlatan on the first day. But we had to pretend otherwise or we'd get fired. He's a good mask maker and sculptor and he should've stuck to it. But he has an inflated ego. Like I said, he's in love with himself, man. But some of us would roll our eyes at him behind his back. The actors and actresses weren't at ease with him. "

I was almost glad to hear that, not because I enjoyed hearing Derrick being put down but because I was glad other people in the business weren't always wearing blinders where he was concerned.

"See you at the next convention gig," Gary said. "I've already got my van loaded up and I'm buggin' outta here."

"See you, Gary," I muttered disconsolately.

I tossed my empty beer bottle into a trash can, then continued to sit there in a kind of hopeless inertia. It had always aggravated me that people like Derrick Hubbara got away with being careerists and charlatans -- but now, thanks to what had been said to me by his buddy Gary and his angry, bitter ex-wife, I was struggling with the possibility that he may have sexually groomed his own daughter to start molesting her and was now carrying on with his niece. The mere thought of an adult venting his lusts on children was utterly repulsive to me. I had seen a clip on tabloid television of lawyers in suits and ties headed into a federal courthouse to openly advocate for a group calling itself "Lamda: The Man-Boy Love Association." Like hate speech, it couldn't be prosecuted unless it could be proven that what it advocated actually got carried out.

In America, one of the prices we paid for our freedoms was that even the worst uses of free speech could not be stifled. Sexual peccadilloes of the usual kind were often tolerated if not condoned or even sometimes lauded. When one of my favorite authors, Norman Mailer, was asked on camera why Bill Clinton's poll numbers went way up after he was accused of sexual assault, Mailer said, "Well, most people have sex lives that couldn't bear any sort of scrutiny, so they don't want anybody else's to be scrutinized either."

I despaired over the fact that there didn't seem to be any limits anymore. Over my long career I had often been appalled by the extent people to which people would give up their principles in favor of their aspirations. It was true in all walks of life but was probably even more true in show business and politics where career viability often hung by a thread, making people frantic about their ability to hang on. I tried to believe that I was a highly principled person in spite of the kinds of movies I made. I refused to become bitter over the fact that I had tried to make more uplifting or at more culturally important movies, but the industry wouldn't let me. I had come tantalizingly close with *Dealey Plaza* and it had gotten me caught in the undertow of a heinous double murder, which was bad enough without the kinds of sexual implications I was now hearing about. I couldn't help hoping that some of the things I had been told today were complete and utter poppycock.

CHAPTER 12

Vito and I read the autopsy report in Captain Devereux's office and it verified that Darby Coltrane's identity had been confirmed through dental comparisons. He had a bullet hole in his forehead and bullet fragments in his skull. There was no soot found in his lungs, which meant that he was no longer alive when the fire took hold.

The most disturbing new revelation was an outline of a naked body where the genital area was circled and inside the circle was a handwritten note in capitals that said: *Genitals crudely removed.*

"Genitals crudely removed," Vito murmured. "What do we make of that? I don't mean to ask a dumb question but..."

Captain Devereux told us, "I asked the M.E. about it and he said the victim's genitals were sliced off. At the crime scene we saw that his midsection was burnt and charred more than the rest of him, but we didn't speculate. Neither did the guys with the body bag. They had a hard enough time getting his remains into it. They all had Vick's smeared under their nostrils. CSI is still at work in what's left of Coltrane's house. Maybe they'll find something that can help us."

"I'm thinking it's a revenge murder coupled with sexual sadism," Vito said. "The darkest side of human behavior, Joy. Unfortunately, there will be other cases where you'll see more of it if you hang in with me."

I wanted to show him and the captain that I could think logically even in the face of such things so I said, "It doesn't comport with the M.O. in Lance Goldman's case. There's no

74

evidence of sexual deviancy and no one has tried to point us in that direction."

"That's a good point," Vito said. "We need to find out if Coltrane might've had a spurned lover or any other kind of rival, male or female. Maybe he was into the S&M scene."

Captain Devereux said, "I asked Victoria if Coltrane was gay and she said she kind of thought he was, but he was closeted. Unusual these days when people feel they can come out, but after all he was working with kids, and he wouldn't have kept his job long if a bunch of parents had raised a fuss."

"Talk about a motive," Vito said. "Lots of people think anybody who does bad stuff with kids deserves whatever he gets."

Captain Devereux rubbed his eyes and said, "Things are getting crazier and crazier, if you ask me. We've got a lady who was living the American dream in Woodland Hills, but she's been behind bars for two years awaiting trial for murder and conspiracy on her own husband, a rich celebrity chef with a TV show. He was bewitched by her. She could do no wrong in his eyes. She set the murder up so she'd be shopping at a Target store and her twelve-year-old daughter would discover Daddy's body after Mommy's lover stabbed the poor guy seventeen times out by the swimming pool. The killer drove away in the husband's Porsche, then abandoned it, and we found blood drops in it and ran them for DNA -- and got a match. And dig this -- the bastard was the wife's racquet ball coach! And he had a sheet. He did six years in prison in Arizona for lewd and lascivious behavior with a minor. You can't make this stuff up. And it just keeps coming, worse than ever."

Vito said, "Cop suicides are way up. I don't think it was such a job hazard back when I first started."

"It wasn't," said Captain Devereux.

We all fell silent for a moment. Then I said to Vito, "We better get my dad out here, don't you think? Unless he's turned up something that warrants him staying in Pittsburgh."

CHAPTER 13

Joy gave me a call and Vito joined in on speakerphone. First they asked me if I had anything that required their immediate attention, and I said, "Nothing earthshaking. Just a lot of stuff tumbling through my brain as a result of run-ins with Derrick Hubbara and his daughter and his ex-wife."

"So you did get next to him?" Vito asked.

"As close as I'll probably ever get. He's weirder than I thought. Am I staying here or coming out there?"

"Looks like you should book a flight," Vito said.

Joy said, "Dad, we have a lot going on all of a sudden. Two murders that could be related to our case. And right here in L.A."

"You're saying you need me there, honey?"

In falsetto, Vito said, "Yes, *sweetheart.*"

I told him, "You're not a honey you're a sour old man. I was calling my daughter honey, not you."

"I think Vito's a honey," Joy said. "You both are."

"See that, smartass," said Vito.

"Who are the vics?" I asked.

"A guy named Darby Coltrane and a passerby who got shot for trying to call 9-1-1 and report the fire."

"Oh-oh, I know him," I said, feeling like I had just gotten smacked in the face.

Joy said, "Who, Dad?"

"Darby Coltrane. There can't be someone else by that name. I don't know him well, but he worked on my last sequel because Derrick Hubbara recommended him. He's a dialogue coach for some of the kids starring in *Zombie Hunterz*, the TV show Hubbara's daughter is in under the name Jennifer Huber. I used him as a continuity person and he did an okay job."

"Why does Hubbara's name keep coming up in these murders?" Vito said, not expecting an answer. "I know the movie business is somewhat incestuous, but it's starting to creep me out."

I said, "Hubbara's daughter is trying her best to behave like a tramp, judging by how she came off at the convention. There were some pretty bizarre things going on, I can tell you that much."

After a moment of silence, Vito said once again that it'd be best if I headed to L.A. to work with him and Joy rather than them rejoining me in Pittsburgh.

"Shit, I hate to fly," I muttered. "Especially three thousand miles -- and worse if I can't get a direct flight."

"Suck it up," Vito said. "Fly the Friendly Skies."

"That's an oxymoron."

The only flight I ever truly enjoyed was my very first one after I got out of the army and was coming home. As an aspiring writer, I craved the experience. I was in a hurry to become more worldly. But pretty much right after that being on a big droning cigar-shaped thing totally outside of my control became infinitely monotonous and boring.

But luckily I booked a flight without a layover for the next morning, a Wednesday, and after five hours of no sleep even though I tried, Vito and Joy met me at Lax in a white van that belonged to Lance International Pictures but was going incognito, without a logo. "Glad to ditch the friendly skies," I mumbled as I climbed into it.

"We're gonna take you to a nice Chinese lunch," Vito said from behind the wheel. That way we can catch you up on the situation here and you can unwind from the jet lag."

78

"I'm sure that if you two know the place the food is gonna be great," I said. "It'll make me feel like a real person again, Back when I used to produce TV spots I liked to get to my office early enough to give myself some down time before the crew would arrive. I'd stop at the Mickey D's and grab a coffee and something to munch on, then sit at my desk for a few minutes of tranquility all by myself. I used to tell the crew it was all downhill after my egg McMuffin."

"It's one of their only good things," Joy said.

"Yep," said Vito.

After our delicious non-McDonald's meal of wonton soup and egg rolls, beef with oyster sauce, mushu pork and vegetable fried rice, we went straight to the Beverly Hilton and I checked myself in and dumped my luggage, then joined Joy and Vito in a conference room they had been keeping on reserve the whole time they were here. They asked for a coffee setup to be brought in and we helped ourselves to it while Joy opened her laptop and positioned it so the three of us could see the screen if we all sat on the same side of the conference table. Then she called up Season One of *Zombie Hunterz* after we decided to watch the pilot first and hope it was all we would need to sit through for our purposes. It was already into its third season.

The title and opening credits came on to the accompaniment of a heart-pounding song called *Beat 'em or Burn 'Em* scoring an "action-packed montage" -- as a blurb might say -- of a bunch of kids in a knock-down drag-out battle with a pack of ghastly ghouls smashing their way into a suburban home. Three ghouls came in through a door hanging sideways on its hinges and

two more were crawling in through a shattered window as the kids puffed themselves up for a

brawl. The four of them, two boys and two girls, were extraordinarily adept in Tae Kwando and ju jitsu, and the zombies ended up being vanquished by kicks to the head, necks twisted and broken, and heads bashed in -- all pulled off in a non-gory fashion utilizing sound effects and discreet edits tailored for TV.

Picture and sound dissolved and segued to a peaceful suburban neighborhood with birds chirping and I didn't get to see anymore of the movie because Joy turned it off. "Ready to scan through some of the DVD Extras?" she asked me and Vito.

We both said yes and she moved the cursor down a list of screening choices and clicked on *Behind-the-Scenes*. She let it play normally at first, then hit fast-forward, but slow enough that we could still make out who we were seeing on-camera. When she came upon a medium close-up of Darby Coltrane I said, "That's him," and she slowed the picture back to normal play. He had in his left hand a script that was folded back on itself and standing next to him, almost hip to hip, was one of the boy actors whose face we had seen in a yellow computer-generated circle in the opening credits. I remembered his name: Ryan Grace. He was about twelve years of age and he had an impish smile and a raft of blonde hair he constantly had to push out of his blue eyes. Coltrane kept nudging him with his right arm and intermittently laid his hand on young Ryan's shoulder.

Throughout the Behind-the-Scenes clips, which were sprightly narrated, Darby Coltrane seemed to focus his efforts as dialogue coach much more on the photogenic young boys than on the young female actresses. And he couldn't seem to keep his hands off of them. And we spotted a couple of shots where Jennifer Huber appeared in the background, scowling at him.

When the DVD Extra came to an end Vito said, "Well, what do you two have to say? I think there's little doubt that our friend Darby had a thing for young boys. And the ones we saw were obviously cast because of their charisma and athleticism."

"And their pre-pubescent charm for a guy like Coltrane," Joy said.

"Amen. And somebody probably killed him because of it," I said.

"Let's not jump ahead of ourselves," Vito cautioned. "Joy, are you up for downloading and printing out the cast list, the crew list, every other list that pertains, and starting to dig into them? We need a lot more information before we can start making any moves."

I ventured to say, "I don't think we have to wait any longer before we question Jenny Hubbara. I told you how snotty she acts around her father. I wouldn't mind putting some heat on her."

Vito said, "That's exactly what we don't want to do yet, Dave. We need to get all our ducks in a row. If we jump on Jenny too soon she can put a bug in her co-stars' ears and they can come up with matching stories."

"Okay, I stand corrected," I told him.

Joy said, "Attaway, Dad! Come clean right away, that's what you always taught me."

"I hope that's not all you learned from me," I said. "And I hope you realize I never had to do a whole lot of coming clean."

"You're as pure as the driven slush," Vito said.

CHAPTER 14

While I was still in L.A. with Vito and my dad, it happened to be *Monsterpalooza* weekend, one of the best of those kinds of events, and it was always held in a major hotel right in Hollywood. It was much larger than the Pittsburgh Horror Convention because so many movie celebrities were readily available and didn't have to travel long distances. The promoter didn't have to pay for flights and hotel rooms except for the relatively few who flew in from out of town. So I phoned the promoter on my dad's behalf, and he said there was a last-minute cancellation and he'd be glad to give us the booth. Dad and I knew that Derrick Hubbara was going to be there and figured that if I got a chance to approach him, I might get more out of him than Dad had because he had eyed me up on quite a few occasions.

"I'm gonna give it a shot," I told Vito, "even though he might very well stonewall me since he knows I work for you."

"What's that brand new saying? Nothing ventured, nothing gained." Vito quipped.

You're so original!" I told him.

My dad already did a good job of portraying how these events unfold, so I'm going to cut to the chase. At Monsterpalooza I never once saw Derrick and his daughter hanging out together and they both snubbed me anytime I came near them. I split most of my time either circulating around to see if I could pick up any scuttlebutt or else helping my dad at his booth. He said his lines were much longer than in

Pittsburgh, which was not surprising since it was a much denser population area and like I said, it was Hollywood.

I strolled nonchalantly past Derrick Hubbara's booth quite a few times, pretending not to look his way, and couldn't help noticing he was being surly with quite a few of his fans after they had spent an hour or more in his line and were spending their hard-earned cash. He had a constant scowl on his face. While I was sitting behind my dad's tables at least a half dozen of the autograph seekers openly said that Derrick Hubbara was a sourpuss, an ungrateful egotist or worse and they wouldn't ever stand in line for him again.

In the final hour of the show, on Saturday, Gary Chelton, one of my dad's colleagues, came up to us and said, "Are you hip to why Hubbara has such a hair up his ass?"

Dad and I rolled our eyes and shrugged.

Gary said, "All of his stash was stolen. Not his dope, his cash. He told me about it. He says it was all of his unreported take from half a year's conventions. The dude doesn't even know how much -- he just comes home and tosses wads of it into his safe without bothering to count it. He says when he finally does count it he wants to be pleasantly surprised by how much of a bonanza it is. But now it's all gone. Well, it's not *all* gone, whoever took it left him three ones like you would tip at a Wendy's or something."

"Does he have any idea who took it," my dad asked.

I perked up for the answer, half hoping it might have some bearing on our two murder cases.

"Nope," Gary answered. "He says he must've left the safe hanging open 'cause he was stoned when he crawled into bed. "

"That sounds implausible," my dad said.

"I agree," Gary said, leaning forward so as to be discreet. "I'd guess it was his daughter or her boyfriend Giorgio or both of them, but I'd never put that out there. Derrick wants to believe it wasn't them, so let him. He's going around blaming himself. But Jennifer would have had the easiest access to the combination, unless Derrick conked out with one of his one-night stands after opening the safe to impress her."

"What about his niece?" I dared to ask.

"You know about that?" Gary muttered, miffed at himself. "I should never have opened my mouth about her." He cast a sour look at my dad.

"I had to tell Vito and Joy," Dad said by way of apology. "In case it may have a bearing on what happened to Lance Goldman."

"Yeah, yeah," Gary mumbled sarcastically. "I guess I'll forgive you, Dave, but you better put me on your next movie." He walked away sullenly.

That night, instead of going to the VIP party, I spent a couple of hours digging into Jenny Huber's boyfriend, Giorgio, in case the two of them had anything to do with robbing Derrick's safe, and on the chance that, if so, there might be a tie-in to the murder cases.

Looking at head shots of Giorgio Luviano online, I wasn't surprised to see that my dad's description of him was spot on, and I reminded myself that, after all, Dad was a screenwriter, accustomed to putting accurate character descriptions down on paper. Giorgio's stats were: 5 foot, four and 125. He had thick, wavy black hair and perfectly sculpted sideburns down to his jaws. I thought he was handsome in a gangbanger sort of way.

An item in his thumbnail bio hit me with a jolt. He claimed to be a protégé of armaments specialist Jose Della Cruz, the same guy Derrick Hubbara had beat up when Della Cruz was a prop master on one of Hubbara's movies.

I clicked on the link to Giorgio's website. In splashy red calligraphy it said: *GIORGIO LUVIANO MASTER OF DEADLY WEAPONS*. A slightly built little guy in a black leather jacket with the sleeves torn off, he was brandishing an assault rifle, pointing it straight at the camera. He had pipe-stem arms covered with tattoos, which made me think of all the wimpy, non-athletic, picked-on kids who mowed their classmates down with that same kind of rapid-fire banana-clipped gun. The banner was bordered by a chain of swastikas that alternated with photos of Lugers, knives, machetes, maces, burp guns, spears, axes and whips. It was Luger, swastika, knife, swastika, machete, swastika, like that all the way.

Here it was again: Nazi implications on the banner. Plus, a Luger had figured in the kidnapping and deaths of Lance Goldman and his driver. And several years ago, my dad and Vito had helped take down the main installation of the Aryan Confederacy, which was a key episode in my dad's book and proposed movie, and the torched limo and burnt bodies had been found there.

Stunned by all these implications, I pushed my chair back and used my cell phone to reach Vito and my dad, itching to tell them what I had discovered.

CHAPTER 15

I didn't man my booth at Monsterpalooza on Sunday morning. Instead I went with Joy and Vito to Captain Devereux's office. Now we could see that his hair was thinning but not totally bald. He was in civvies, navy blue trousers, a tan short-sleeved shirt and Reeboks. As soon as we got there he offered us Panera coffee and bagels with cream cheese and we gratefully accepted since we hadn't dallied at our hotel. The four of us sat around a coffee table near the windows in his office. The day outside was bright and rainless, as is usual in Los Angeles, which made me think of that song, *It Never Rains in California.*

Joy had opened her laptop even as we were munching and sipping and she turned the screen toward Captain Devereux so he could see Giorgio Luviano's garishly bannered web page.

After allowing the captain a long moment of staring at Luviano's badass pose and the border of weapons and swastikas Vito said, "A real charmer, isn't he?"

"What a fucked up little shit!" the captain barked. "His so-called mentor, Jose Della Cruz, will be here in about twenty minutes, if he keeps his word. If he doesn't I'll put out a BOLO on him and bust his ass for making me give up my afternoon tennis game."

Vito said, "I don't expect you gave him any hint as to why you need to talk to him again."

"You expect correctly," said the captain.

86

"I have to give a lot of credit to my daughter," I said. "She might have turned up a whole new direction to take our two separate murder cases."

"I've stopped thinking of them as separate," Joy said.

"Me, too," Vito agreed.

Captain Devereux nodded grimly.

"Let's go over what we have so far," Vito said. "You take the lead, Joy. You've got the screen and the keyboard."

Flipping from one screen to another as needed, Joy got us started summing up the two cases, one on the West coast and one on the East coast, that none of us were now regarding as separate. We agreed on the similarities that seemed evident:

(1) At least two of the victims -- Lance Goldman and Darby Coltrane -- were connected quite strongly with Lance International Pictures.

(2) At least three persons of interest -- Derrick Hubbara, Giorgio Luviano and Jose Della Cruz -- were connected in various ways with Lance Goldman and/or his company, Lance International Pictures.

(3) Two potentially additional persons of interest were Hubbara's niece, Carla, his ex-wife Leona, and his daughter, stage name Jenny Huber.

(4) There could be persons unknown still not under our radar.

(5) There were similarities between the two murder cases, East Coast and West coast.

Arson was a powerful element in both. Also both carried hints, whether real or manufactured, of
some kind of connection, maybe even possibly an homage, to the Aryan Confederacy

(6) Both Vito Martinelli and I had had catastrophic or nearly catastrophic run-ins with
the Aryan Confederacy in the recent past.

While we were discussing all this Captain Devereux's desk phone rang. He picked up, listened, and told us that Jose Della Cruz was being held in an interrogation room. He led us down a hallway and let Vito go into the room with him while Joy and I would watch and listen through an observation window. We knew the interview would be taped.

Della Cruz was wearing jeans and a T-shirt, as before, he looked more abashed than I expected from the way Vito and Joy had described him during his first interview. I thought maybe being in the Los Angeles Police Headquarters made him more leery.

Captain Devereux didn't read him his rights right away. He and Vito stayed disarmingly polite during the preliminaries -- but as soon as they mentioned Giorgio Luviamo it provoked an outburst.

"That stinking little piece of shit!" Jose erupted. "He better not come around me!"

"He claims you as his mentor -- on his web page," Captain Devereux said.

"Mentor my ass! He stayed in my prop master class for a about week and a half before he started bitching that he didn't get hired anywhere! I told him I paid my dues for six years till I finally got my first break -- as a volunteer. I had to prove myself over and over."

"Then how does he get away with calling you his mentor?" Vito asked.

"Because in many ways Hollywood is a big fat scam!" Della Cruz blurted. "Like Derrick Hubbara -- a fucking charlatan! That's all he is. Lance Goldman bought into him -- and look what Lance got for it! No good deed goes unpunished!"

"Vito said, "When my colleague and I first talked with you in Victoria Goldman's office, you told us you settled a lawsuit against Hubbara after he claimed you left a dumdum round in a prop pistol. Do you still stick to that story?"

"Damn right I do! And don't forget it was a false accusation, which he had to admit in the settlement."

Vito said, "Okay. But if it was a false accusation and he knew it was false and eventually admitted it, then what was his real reason for jumping you when you least expected it and putting you in the hospital?"

"I don't know," Della Cruz said. "Other than he's a genuine fourteen carat asshole. Just like that fucked-up kid, Giorgio."

Neither Captain Devereux nor Vito Martinelli got much more that seemed pertinent out of Jose Della Cruz. They dismissed him and motioned me and Joy into the interrogation room, and after a brief discussion we all agreed he probably shouldn't be considered a prime person of interest any longer. We would still keep him on the back burner, but wouldn't waste a whole lot of energy on him from here on out.

The next step was to talk to Giorgio Luviano. But we couldn't find him. We used the resources Joy had turned up on him and Captain Devereux used his own sources which we thought would work better, but we didn't get any immediate results and the captain ordered a BOLO to be put out on him. Then we tried to track down Derrick Hubbara's daughter, Jennifer, thinking they might be together, but we had no luck doing that either and for the moment we were all antsy and frustrated.

Finally, I said, "Don't you think for the time being it might be for the best, guys? I mean not doing anything to alert either one of them and put them on guard. We should come at them

in a roundabout way, talk to some of their friends and associates first. Jennifer's co-stars even."

Joy said, "Yeah, I think you're right, Dad."

Vito said, "But we had better move quickly. We all feel there are two or more killers working as a team and they've already killed four people. I don't get the feeling they're gonna stop."

"We don't know the motive," I said. "If sexual deviancy is in play, as it seems to be with Darby Coltrane, why would Lance Goldman have been the first victim? We don't have any indication he was that way. That's where the two cases don't seem to match up."

"Maybe he was first only because they happened to be where he was headed," said Captain Devereux. "Easy for them to lie in wait. Plus, they were playing off of the neo-Nazi angle."

Vito said, "Lying in wait is considered a special circumstance in Pennsylvania. It makes them eligible for the death penalty."

"That's good," said the captain. "I'd gladly extradite them if we end up arresting them here and putting them in shackles. But to do that we have to figure out who they are."

CHAPTER 16

Carla Barresi was working at a kiosk in one of the main corridors of Monroeville Mall, where the George A. Romero movie *Dawn of the Dead* was filmed. She was a rabid horror fan from a small town where nothing much ever happened, so she was thrilled when she got hired to work in such an iconic environment. The skating rink Romero made famous was gone, replaced by a food court, but she liked knowing where it had been and enjoying her lunch break there on most days, on the very location where Romero's zombies had once been filmed.

Her first cousin, Derrick Hubbara, had never worked on any of Romero's movies, though he had certainly tried hard to get hired as a stunt man, a production assistant, a lowly grip, even a hair dresser -- whatever it took -- but none of those old dreams had come true. That was back when he hadn't yet gotten his big break. Later, after he got famous, he had rubbed shoulders with Mr. Romero but by then he didn't need Romero anymore. They were colleagues. Equals. Yet *not* equals because Derrick was a lot richer. Which of them was the most talented? Carla didn't dare guess. But she knew it often didn't matter in the entertainment business. Her cousin was riding high, that's for sure, and that was the be all and the end all in the biz.

Carla was still working at the Sprint cell phone kiosk because he didn't want her to quit. He said he would continue to respect her and care a lot for her if she remained financially independent, able to earn her own money and keep her own apartment. Sometimes she was scared he didn't want her around him all the time, but she was even more scared to harbor that detrimental thought. On top of it all, she felt like she should be wearing a scarlet "A" for what she was doing with her first cousin.

Two years ago Derrick had come to a family reunion picnic in Kennywood Park, which once again happened to be a place where George Romero had filmed scenes from some of his movies, making use of the screeching but colorful roller coaster rides, the merry-go-rounds and so on, even a section called Kiddy Land, where some of Carla's cousins would take their pre-school children so the other adults wouldn't have to bother with them.

Derrick had arrived by himself and had stayed in the picnic table area, eating and drinking with the other family members, not bothering with any of the rides, and Carla had stared mooney-eyed at him, averting her eyes anytime he looked in her direction, scared to say boo to him because he was so famous and she was a nobody. In fact she thought she was worse than a nobody because she was a failure with two broken marriages and no children. She had always wanted children, she would've loved having two or more to take to Kiddy Land today like some of her relatives were doing with their children, and she felt crushed by disappointment that she would probably never have any of her own. She was twenty-three years old, far too young to feel the ticking of her biological clock, yet she felt it anyway.

All of her family members and extended family members at the annual reunion were unrelentingly Catholic. They were all certain that the mere thought of doing anything sexually inappropriate with a blood relative would condemn them to hell. Yet that was where Carla first began to be enticed into a life of mortal sin.

She didn't think Derrick was paying the least attention to her, therefore she felt herself blushing when he walked up to

92

her as she was sitting under a tree all by herself and asked her if she would show him where the Old Mill was. He said he couldn't remember. He wanted to take a ride through it because it had been his favorite thing back when his grade school picnic was always held here.

"So was mine," Carla said, which she instantly felt was a stupid thing to say, because every school in the county always held its school picnics in Kennywood Park.

Derrick laughed, so she laughed too, because he didn't seem to be making fun of her, though he did seem to be treating her like a teenager or a silly young girl who had not yet attained his own level of worldly intelligence and experience. But he seemed to like her. If she dared to believe that.

She had a feeling that he actually totally remembered exactly where the Old Mill was, because how could anyone who loved it ever forget it? It was very spooky, even on the outside. Ogres and monsters leered from the cobwebbed windows. She and Derrick had to stand in line because there were always plenty of people anxious to get in, yet some of them were already scared, nearly trembling --- especially the prepubescent girls. She knew some were only pretending to be scared, though, working themselves up to snuggling with their boyfriends.

Standing in line, Derrick said to Carla, "This is the ride that made me want to help make horror movies. I remember going through in the total darkness when suddenly there would be a loud shriek that would make me jump -- then the display of Bloody Mary would be all lit up with the executioner holding a bloody axe and her head in a bloody basket. I would use up most of my tickets getting back in line and going through in one of the boats again and again."

Carla was overawed that he was confiding his memories only to her. She was surprised that none of the adolescent boys and girls recognized him -- then she realized that none of them were paying attention to him or her; they were too anxious and too titillated by the thought of necking, grabbing feels and French kissing in the semi-darkness and intermittent stark brightness they were about to experience.

When it was their turn to go through, they climbed into one of the garishly painted boats, which were vaguely designed to resemble a half-hearted miniature replica of a Viking vessel. It had wooden seats for six people. Like all the other boats, it wasn't really floating on the twisting channel of water that wound through the Old Mill; it was being pulled along on mechanized rollers beneath the surface. But the pushed that realization out of her mind so she could buy into the illusion.

The first loud shriek occurred with a great deal of reverberation, and before their very eyes stood Count Dracula biting into the neck of a Victorian damsel in a lacy gown. Dracula was fully clothed, lying on top of her, yet the scene was erotic, and even more so because he was sucking her blood.

Derrick had his arm around her now, and by the time they came to the panorama of Bloody Mary his hand was between her legs, his fingers stroking her. She whimpered and softly told him to stop, but he didn't, and she gave in to the sensations.

Her mind was in a fog and she did not know how much it should matter that they were

related. After all, he was not going to penetrate her. So what was really the harm in it?

They were both wearing tight jeans, and he put her hand on his penis, and it was straining against the fabric, so she rubbed it, as he was doing to her.

She knew what they were doing was wrong, but they both climaxed as another shriek blasted out at them, masking their barely restrained moans of pleasure and the Wolf Man glowered at them, baring his fangs…

CHAPTER 17

The public's reaction to the double murder on the West Coast was different than the overall reaction to the double murder on the East Coast. Panic didn't take hold in Southwestern Pennsylvania, but in Hollywood, it was a different story. Lance Goldman and Darby Coltrane were both affiliated with a movie studio, which gave rise to a general fear that perhaps nobody in the biz was actually safe.

This onslaught of fear was of course greatest among staff and stars of Lance International Pictures. Accordingly, the parents or guardians of the young actors in the TV series, *Zombie Kidz*, balked against any notion of letting their children be questioned by murder investigators. In an effort to soothe the public, Captain Devereux held several press conferences to update everyone about the progress of the Darby Coltrane case and to urge folks who knew him, especially those who had worked with him, to come forward with whatever they thought they knew. "Don't automatically rule out anything that occurs to you," the captain said in one of those conferences. "Something that seems trivial could actually be important. And don't let fear stop you from cooperating with law enforcement. That fear will allow the killer or killers to remain on the loose, where as your brave cooperation will allow us to unmask the killers and bring them to justice." But in spite of his admonishments, only the parents of two teenage actors in *Zombie Kidz* gave permission for the police to talk with them, with stipulation that the parents and the parents' attorneys must be present.

In light of all this, Vito, Joy and I met with Captain Devereux after the third of his press conferences to try to figure out how best to deploy ourselves. "Well, my Los Angeles police force obviously has no shortage of detectives even though they all carry an overwhelming case load," the captain started out saying. "One thing that hasn't changed is it's still a two-pronged investigation. It seems to me that we should treat it as such. In other words, I can take charge here, and you three can head back to Pennsylvania where both cases started."

"That makes sense," Vito acknowledged, "but to a certain extent we might be twiddling our thumbs because we've reached a dead end back there, unless something else happens."

"And it might," the captain said succinctly. "As it also might in my jurisdiction. Why don't you talk with your guy down south from you?"

"Sheriff Boyce," Joy supplied.

"Yes, Boyce," said Captain Devereux. "You've already got a good team of very capable people, and I've seen that. And I've certainly got a good team right here. We can share every key item either team turns up. That's the way I see it."

I turned toward Vito and said, "How do you see it? And you, Joy?"

Joy said, "The captain makes total sense, don't you think, Dad?"

I waited for Vito to speak his mind before I did. He said, "Yes, I have to agree with the captain. We don't need to be nosing around in his territory. I'll explain it to Victoria so she sees the wisdom in it."

"I know her well," Captain Devereux said. "She's a sensible person. I'll prime her for your phone call if you want me to."

"Well, she's my client," said Vito. "So let me break it to her first. I'll do it tactfully."

"You? Tactful? Are you sure, Vito?" Joy said, teasing him.

"Hey, I'm Mister Tactful," he said, smirking..

Captain Devereux said, "As far as those so-called zombie kids go, so far I've only got permission from the parents of two of them, Ryan Grace and Faye Curtis. I'd very much like it if the three of you could observe -- you know, discreetly, from behind glass -- when I have them come in with their parents and attorneys. That way you'll hopefully have a bit more insight before you head back to Pittsburgh."

"We'd like that, too," Vito said. "How soon can it occur?"

"Ryan Grace is already scheduled for tomorrow morning, and Faye Curtis will be here in the afternoon."

"No results yet on Giorgio Luviano's whereabouts?"

"Nope. I don't think he's still in L.A. My men are good and some sharp-eyed patrolman would've spotted him. But wherever he is he's probably with Jenny Huber because we can't find her either."

CHAPTER 18

Now that we had our ducks in a row after doping out a game plan with Captain Devereux, I decided that I should use the rest of that day's working hours to meet with my agent, Devin Lockhart. I hadn't spoken with him since a couple of weeks after Lance Goldman's murder and he deserved to be brought up to date with as much as I could tell him without risking a leak that could blow both investigations.

We decided to have a quick take-out meal at five o'clock in his office because after that he had to "take a meeting" about a script deal for another of his clients.

Waiting for burgers and fries to be brought in, rather than Chinese or Mexican, which would've been messy, I gave Devin a rundown. Then, as any hardnosed agent would, he asked, "How is this going to affect your best interests? Will *Dealey Plaza* remain dead in the water?"

"Unfortunately, I believe it will," I answered.

"Too bad, maybe I can find a way to resuscitate it," he mused. "In fact now that there's actually a screenplay for the pilot, I'll get with Victoria and ask her to revert all rights. Not that I expect to place it elsewhere with any degree of immediacy -- because nobody else ever got as excited about it as Lance did, and she probably won't either."

"She might," I offered. "After all, as one of his top execs, she went along with him on what he wanted to do with it. But if by some miracle you can place it elsewhere, I won't be stuck with Derrick Hubbara as the director."

"How deeply is he connected with these murders?" Devin asked.

But just then there was a knock on his office door and his secretary stepped in with bags of burgers and fries. So we portioned it all out and opened it up at his coffee table, and the secretary left, then came back with bottled water for each of us as we started to dig in. Then, after she went out the door again, I answered the question from Devin that had been left dangling in the air and even elaborated on it.

"At this point I don't know exactly how Derrick is connected, nor his daughter, his ex-wife or the woman he's taken up with, who seems to be his niece, for God's sake."

"His niece?" Devin said, startled and with his mouth full.

"That's what I've been told. But it might be empty gossip. Joy is trying to find out."

"Well, it didn't hurt Jerry Lee Lewis way back when, and the whole country is way more liberal nowadays," Devin said. "Hubbara's career is going to keep on keeping on unless he gets convicted of murder. But so far there's no proof he murdered anybody."

"He might not get convicted even if he did," I said. "Look at O.J. His wife's blood drops were in his driveway and the bloody glove fit him! It was shriveled like any leather glove will be if it's soaked in a liquid -- like blood for instance -- and then dries. Plus O.J. kept his fingers stiff when he tried it on. He suckered the jury because they *wanted* to be suckered. Johnny Cochran kept yapping if it doesn't fit you must acquit -- *bullshit!"*

Devin said, "But on the other hand, what's-his-name *didn't* get away with it. That nutty looking guy with a stupid wig who made hit records. The Wall of Sound -- that was his claim to fame, wasn't it?"

"Yeah. His name is Phil Spector," I said. "He didn't apparently think it was a no-no to shoot an actress right in his own living room."

"It's a hazard to be a famous young woman these days," said Devin. "Obsessed fans show up at their doorstep and stab them to death or gun them down. Nobody is safe out here anymore, even with bodyguards."

CHAPTER 19

On Monday afternoon, Carla Barresi froze when she saw
Jenny Hubbara coming toward her as she stood behind the
glass counter of her Sprint kiosk at Monroeville Mall. Here
comes trouble, big trouble, she thought to herself, wishing she
could make herself invisible so Jenny would walk right by her.
But Jenny didn't. And for some odd reason she was smiling
instead of sneering. Her hair was back to her natural brunette,
not crazy shades of pink or red or chartreuse or whatever. And
she wasn't dressed like a teenage floozy, a wild girl with rings
in her lips and eyebrows. She was wearing a pink blouse and a
blue skirt. So sedate. So innocent seeming. She came right up
to the glass counter and said, "Hi, Carla. Don't be scared of me.
From now on I'm going to be nice to you."

Carla's eyes widened and she said, "What brought that on?"

"It's time for me to start being more mature. My career will
be going nowhere if I don't succeed in changing my image. I
realize I won't be able to portray a precocious teenybopper for
much longer. Like Judy Garland. MGM made her wear a
leather thingy to crush her breasts flat because they didn't want
her to ever grow up and stop playing a cute kid."

Suspiciously Carla said, "Come on, what do you want from
me, Jenny? I know you're not being nice to me for no reason."

With a warm, ingratiating look on her face, Jenny said,
"I've come to a decision that if my dad likes you I have to like
you too. I can't keep upsetting him. He has a career to worry
about too. He's entitled to his own choice of girlfriends."

"Is that what he calls me? His girlfriend?" Carla said hopefully.

"Yes, but you know what you're doing is a sin, don't you?"

Carla felt her face turn red, and she couldn't think of anything to say that would make sense. So she said, "What makes you think I'm having sex with him?"

"Because I know my dad. He wants to have sex with *every* woman. It's just one of his quirks. He thinks society's rules don't apply to him. But if I'm turning over a new leaf, so can you. I'm going to confession tomorrow and I'm taking communion on Sunday. Want to come with me? If you can get yourself into a state of grace, it will be easier to leave my father and make a brand-new life for yourself. Isn't that what the church teaches?"

"Surely you can't be serious!" Carla blurted. "I think you have something up your sleeve, Jenny. But I've actually been thinking about going back to God and begging his forgiveness, and I'm not ashamed to tell you that."

"You should follow the dictates of your conscience," Jenny intoned. "I already talked to Father Mario about my own intentions, and he was very encouraging. As well as he should be if he's found his true calling."

Carla was overwhelmed with the possibility of cleansing her conscience and shedding the

guilt that for too long had her paralyzed. She knew in the depths of her soul that she should make a new start, even if Jenny was fooling with her. So she asked, "What time are you going to confession? I can meet you there, and maybe I'll go through with it. But if you don't show up I'll know you're bullshitting me and I'll tell Derrick."

Jenny laughed halfway amused and said, "If you say anything bad about me, he won't believe you. He never has. I'm still his sweet little angel."

"*That's* for sure," Carla agreed dismally, revealing a touch of envy, which embarrassed her for letting it show. But Jenny didn't laugh at her. So she hastily backpedaled, forced a smile and said, "I'll see you at St. Agnes at one o'clock tomorrow afternoon. And I hope you're not just leading me on for reasons of your own. Please don't toy with me, Jenny."

Jenny said "Oh, just lighten up, Carla! Saturday is only four days away. You'll walk out of that church light as air like I know we both did -- when we were little girls taking our First Holy Communion!"

"Oh, boy! If I could ever recapture that feeling!" Carla said.

CHAPTER 20

It was nine o'clock California time that Monday when a sergeant led Ryan Grace, his father and his attorney into an interrogation room where Vito and Captain Devereux were waiting. Joy and I were observing through the one-way glass. As soon as I saw Ryan, I recognized him as the boy Darby Coltrane had appeared to have a thing for, in the tape we had watched of *Zombie Kidz: Behind the Scenes*. He was about three years older now, still with that shock of blonde hair, still with the habit of repeatedly pushing it out of his eyes. He and his father were both wearing tan slacks and golf T-shirts.

Captain Devereux was in his full uniform, minus his formal dark blue jacket with gold insignia on it, and Vito was in a dark suit with a striped tie. It was the decorum they wanted to present because they had figured that the attorney, Cameron Fisk, would be similarly attired, and he was. Fisk bore a demeanor that was rigidly placid, not unfriendly but not antagonistic either.

At least for now. He uncapped the bottled water that was before him and took a sip. Each person in their had his own plastic bottle of it. It was a pressure situation and mouths tended to go dry. Ryan was awkward and fidgety even though he had not been accused of anything and we anticipated that he probably wouldn't be. We thought of him only as a witness, not a culprit

Captain Devereux pressed a button on a small recording device on the interrogation-room's bolted-down table and said, "This interview is being recorded. Today is June 29, 2023. This is Captain Charles Devereux. My colleague is Detective Vito Martinelli. Also present are Ryan Grace, a minor, his father Lucas Grace and their attorney Mr. Cameron Fisk. Please state that you are here of your free will, Ryan."

Ryan started to speak, nothing came out and he fidgeted and cleared his throat.

Attorney Fisk spoke up before the boy could say anything. "As his attorney I will stipulate that he's here of his own free will. But his father has a statement to make. Go ahead, Mr. Grace."

In a confident, well-measured baritone, Mr. Grace, the founder and president of a high-technology company, showed himself to be very articulate as he launched into an outpouring of facts and admissions that none of us had expected to come out so suddenly and devastatingly. Nobody in the room interrupted for fear of interfering with the flow of it. It was as if he were opening a curtain, hitherto a veil of mystery on the two murder cases and doing it with great personal pain to himself and his son.

"Ryan has told me what was being done to him, and I immediately wanted to kill Darby Coltrane if he weren't already dead," Mr. Grace began. "He's been molesting my son for the past three years, and Ryan isn't the only one, he's done it to other young boys and girls. My wife and I are divorced, and I won custody of Ryan, for reasons that don't matter here. But like many men who try to be a good single parent, I also have a successful company to run, and I've been -- and still am -- immersed in it. I believed that Ryan was doing well and didn't require much close supervision by me, because he was being watched over by the entire staff of his TV series and he is such an intelligent and cautious young boy."

Ryan, who had seemed totally struck to silence up until now, managed to say in a near whisper, "Thanks, Dad."

105

His father patted his shoulder and went on. "I know I'm to blame for letting Ryan become a victim. It wasn't as if I was ignorant of how these things happen. I'm Catholic, and I was hit hard by the horrendous sex scandals in the church. I wanted to believe it was only a few bad apples, but it wasn't. It turned out to be systemic. And not just among the Roman Catholic clergy. Predators like Darby Coltrane gravitate to where they can wreak their charms, their patient seductive grooming, on a goodly supply of young prey, boys or girls. They become priests, ministers, scout leaders, whatever it takes for them to get into perfect position to ply their predilections."

He paused for a moment and turned toward his son. "Ryan, would you like to say anything? Go ahead, son, if you're ready. They're going to want to hear from you."

"No, you talk more for now, Dad."

"All right, Son," Mr. Grace said softly. Then, turning toward Vito and Captain Devereux, he went on, in a self-accusatory manner. "I should've wised up. I hate myself for being so obtuse, because the signs were there, I just didn't pay enough attention. Instead of trying to understand and delve deeper, I punished Ryan when his grades went way down and he rebelled against things he used to love doing. He slunk off by himself all the time. I made him stay home and study more. I took things he liked away from him. I even threatened to make him drop out of his acting career if he couldn't get his grades up. I wanted him to go to college but I said I wouldn't pay a dime toward it if he didn't earn at least a partial scholarship."

He paused, took a deep breath and said, "Go ahead, ask a question, if either of you two gentlemen have one."

Vito and Captain Devereux looked toward each other, and the captain nodded, so Vito said, "Mr. Grace, how and when did you start to become aware of what your son was really going through?"

106

"Only three days ago," was his rather stunning answer. "Ryan came to me in my home office and asked if we could have a talk. He looked like he was so weak he might collapse. I told him he looked ill and said maybe we should go into the living room where he could lie down. It was only a week or so since he had a wellness check, and I was scared he was going to tell me he had some kind of debilitating disease -- because that would have explained everything I had been punishing him for -- the falling grades, the antisocial behavior and so on. But instead, that's when he told me what that bastard had been doing to him."

"How long had it been going on?" Vito said. "Either you or your son can answer."

Ryan was at last able to speak up and he said, "Ever since I was eight years old." He turned toward his father. "How explicit should I be?" he asked him.

"Tell what you feel like telling," Mr. Grace said.

"Don't worry, we're totally on your side, and so is everybody here," Attorney Fisk told Ryan. "You have nothing to be ashamed of. None of it was your fault."

Joy and I turned from the one-way glass for a moment and gave each other sad looks.

Ryan was working up the courage to say more.

His father said, "You don't have to endure anymore of this, Son. We've told them what they need to know. We've told them all *we* know. I don't have any idea how it could help solve that predator's murder, and I don't give a damn. I'd like to give whoever did it a medal and a hefty reward."

"I don't blame you," Vito said. "Registered sex offenders! I don't believe sex offenders should be registered anywhere but in their obituaries or on their tombstones. Better yet, their ashes should be scattered to the wind."

"We're sworn to uphold the law, not vigilantism," Captain Devereux flatly reminded.

"I wanted to kill him a thousand times!" Ryan barked out. "I know other kids he did it to. He told me stuff about Jenny Huber too!"

At this, Joy and I perked up.

Ryan's father said, "You never told me anything like that, Son."

"I used to dislike Jenny but now I hate her dad!" Ryan blurted. "Darby knew what her dad was doing to her and he told me if it was okay for them it was okay for him and me. He said whatever felt good was okay to do."

"What did Mr. Coltrane say about Jenny and how did he say he knew about it?" Vito asked. He kept his voice level, but I knew he fervently wanted the answer, and so did we all.

Ryan seemed to sag in his chair. Tears rolled from his eyes and he wiped them with his hand, but more tears flowed.

"It's all right, Son, go on and tell them," his father encouraged.

In a soft, tremulous vice, as if remembering a bad dream, Ryan said, "Darby told me he worked in a movie with Derrick Hubbara and the movie was being shot in Pittsburgh, and there were nights when they drank all night at Derrick's house when Jenny wasn't there. So at one of those times Darby said he got so drunk and foolish he let his guard down and babbled something to the effect that he was no stranger to dark nights. And Derrick knew what Darby meant, that he wasn't out of the closet yet and he liked young kids like me. He said he liked boys or girls, it made no difference to him, we smelled the same and felt the same."

"My God!" Derrick's father couldn't help blurting. But he instantly made himself clam up.

Ryan said, "So when Darby confessed about himself, Derrick wanted to make him feel better, because Derrick was just as drunk as he was, and he got a secretive look on his face and said, "Follow me." And he led Darby upstairs and said,

108

"Look in there, Darby. This is Jenny's bedroom." They stood there for a long while, till it sunk in on Darby that there was no bed in that room. And then Derrick led Darby to another room where there was a large round water bed and said, "This is my bedroom." And both sides of the bed looked slept in, and some of Jenny's personal things were on the nightstand."

This froze all of us, not just everybody in the interrogation room but also Joy and I who were observing.

"Holy shit," Vito finally said.

"It's not evidence, it's hearsay," Captain Devereux pointed out.

"That's correct," said Attorney Fisk. "I don't think my clients have anything to add here. It's up to you now. You two investigators. They've given you plenty to investigate."

"That's for sure, and we're grateful," Captain Devereux said. "You should be proud of yourself, Ryan. You're a brave young man. You didn't deserve what was done to you. None of us can avoid all the evil in this world. But you're going to be okay now. Coming forward like this is going to make it easier for you."

Ryan's father said, "I think we're done here. If your investigation generates any further questions, you can reach us through our attorney, Mr. Fisk. This is a nice afternoon and Ryan and I are heading to my country club for a round of golf - - something we haven't done together for a long time."

As father and son got up to leave, Mr. Fisk said, "I'm staying. I'm Faye Curtis's attorney as well. She and Ryan are close friends."

Joy and I had been standing all this time, antsy at first over what might be about to happen, and later upset over what we were hearing from Ryan Grace and his dad. When they left we plopped into the directors' chairs that had been provided for us and uncapped and took gulps of our bottled water which we had left sitting on a ledge beneath the one-way glass.

Within a couple of minutes, Faye Curtis arrived with her mother, and Joy and I watched and listened as they were introduced by Attorney Fisk to Vito and Captain Devereux as "Mrs. Curtis and her daughter Faye." They sat in the seats vacated by Ryan Grace and his father, and Faye's mom said, "You may call me Helen."

We knew Faye was thirteen and she was looking as uniquely pretty as she had looked in the *Zombie Kidz* pilot, but with a subdued aura about her. Helen didn't appear much older than Faye at first glance; in other words they came off more like sisters than mother and daughter. They were both blondes with shoulder-length hair, and I didn't think Helen was bleaching hers yet. I guessed that she must've given birth at a very young age, maybe as a teenager. They were both wearing colorful sweaters and body-clinging slacks smartly tailored and probably quite costly, perhaps bought on Rodeo Drive.

Captain Devereux said to them, "You already know we've talked with Ryan Grace and his father. We're hoping you both will be as forthcoming as they were so our investigation can move forward on the right track."

"We want to help as much as we can," Helen said. "But we can't help being glad that damned pervert is dead. It's too bad he can only die once. *His* suffering is over unless he's burning in hell, but Faye's suffering continues. She's in counseling and on medication for panic attacks and agoraphobia, which is probably going to end her career. He stole her innocence and neither of us care so much about *career* anymore -- we just want her to get her life back -- to the extent that she still can."

Captain Devereux said, "We know what a brave act it is for you to be here and I want you to know that in helping us you may be helping yourselves more."

Attorney Fisk said, "I agree with that, especially for you, Faye. It's as if you're punishing your abuser by being a survivor and confronting him even though he's dead. It's a way of ridding yourself of his evil spirit or the lingering remnants of it so he can't hurt you anymore."

I had never heard an attorney speak so mystically. It made me wonder if he might be Catholic. I had long ceased being such a strong believer, but I was all for it if it helped Faye to handle her fears.

Joy and I leaned closer toward the one-way glass, keyed up at the prospect of imminent revelations that might be as stunning as what we had heard from Ryan Grace. He had said he and Faye were close friends, which might mean they had both been groomed and preyed upon and had found a way to confide in one another and share each other's pain.

Helen Curtis said, "We have a pretty good idea of what Ryan and his father must have told you -- if the poor boy was able to go through with it. Was he?"

"Yes, he acquitted himself well," said Captain Devereux. "I'm pretty certain he didn't hold anything back. Nobody should ever have to go through anything like that."

"If you're looking for a motive for that creep's murder, I suppose you can stop looking," Helen said bitterly. "I should also think you wouldn't need to look too hard for his killer. And I wish you wuldn't."

"Well, people who take the law into their own hands don't deserve to get away scot free. Not if we can help it. Besides, we think that whoever killed Mr. Coltrane also killed other people who were innocent of the ugly behavior Coltrane indulged in."

"Are you perfectly sure of that?" Helen Curtis shot back at him.

"Not perfectly but reasonably so," Vito cut in. Then he said in his softest and most empathetic manner, "Faye...do you feel ready to talk at least a little bit about how the perpetrator singled you out? Chose you? When he started grooming you, in other words. I'm sorry...I'm trying to be delicate, but these sorts

111

of things are ugly and hurtful, no matter how I might try to couch them in kindness...which I truly feel."

"I can tell you mean that," Helen told him.

"I do," Vito said. "But Faye doesn't need to go any further if she doesn't feel this is the time and place."

"No...I want to," Faye suddenly said, and she began to tell her story, at first in a low and barely discernible tone, which got stronger as she went on. "He...Mr. Coltrane...started by putting me down constantly...right in front of everybody. He'd make snide comments about my clothes or my looks or even the way I delivered my lines. He made me so self-conscious I actually thought I was going to be replaced in the series. But then, after several weeks of this, he took me aside one day and spoke to me in the kindliest way. He put his hand on my shoulder and confided that the reason he was so hard on me was because I was special. He said I was more gifted than the others were. He was tougher on me because he was trying to force me to take stock of myself and not underplay my abilities. He was the dialogue coach for all of us, all of my co-stars, not just me, but he said he'd like to start giving me special attention, but apart from all the others, so no one else would know about it and become jealous or spiteful."

"Where did all this take place?" Vito asked.

"He started driving me home when rehearsals or shootings were over -- "

Helen cut in, saying, "I was so naive I thought it was nice of him. I'm a single mom and I work two jobs."

Faye said, "It's not your fault, Mother. He's utterly charming -- or he was -- whenever he wanted to be."

"I'll never stop blaming myself!" Helen cried out, wiping tears from her eyes, and Faye reached out and took her hand.

Then Faye forced herself to go on. "I want to get this over with, then Mom and I will go home and cry in our bedrooms," she said. "I told you he started taking me home sometimes, and if Mom wasn't there he'd say I needed a massage or something, just to loosen me up before practicing my lines, and at first he'd just rub my neck and shoulders...but one day he went further. And I don't know why, but I didn't stop him. I was scared to. By that time the last thing on earth that I wanted was to lose his belief in me, and his special coaching."

Captain Devereux spoke up right then. "Faye, I think we all understand how you were victimized, and it isn't necessary for you to put yourself through any more of it. It's a good thing Coltrane won't go to trial because you would've been viciously grilled by some defense lawyer trying his damnedest to discredit you. But all of us here are on your side. We're sorry for everything you endured and we appreciate your bravery in being here. I'd just like to cover something that your friend Ryan told us to see if you can confirm it."

"Okay," Faye said. "I'm glad we don't have to keep talking about the other stuff."

"We don't," said the captain. "But Ryan told us some things about Jennifer Huber and Derrick Hubbara. Are you aware of anything...uh...indelicate...that might be going on between the two of them?"

"Ryan told me what Darby Coltrane told him, but neither of us knew whether or not to believe it. Ryan said Darby was drunk and blubbering when he mumbled on about it."

"So Darby never told you personally about any of that? You only heard it second hand from Ryan. Is that right?"

Faye bit her lip and nodded.

"If anything, more of that sort should come to mind, please get in touch with me," the captain said. "It would be very important."

"I still hope it's not true," Faye said, sadly.

Helen said, "I don't want her to have to keep dredging it all up. But if it comes to her awareness of its own accord, in a therapy session for instance, we will certainly let you know, Captain Devereux."

"I can't ask for any more than that. Thank you for being here," the captain said.

"I can't say it's been a pleasure," Helen said grimly, "but we knew we had to do the right thing, and you've been very kind. I think it's going to help us heal."

"I hope you're right, Mom," Faye said hesitantly.

"Please get in touch with me if you need to," said Attorney Fisk to Vito and Captain Devereux. Then he turned toward Faye and Helen, gave them a tight little smile, and escorted them from the captain's office.

When Joy and I came into the office, Vito said, "It's all beginning to tie together. All four of the murders are connected. And the thing that connects them is the molestation issue. That's where the motive lies, even if we're not sure of all the possible entanglements."

Captain Devereux said, "It all appears to come back to Derrick Hubbara somehow. But we know he had no direct part in what was done to Lance Goldman and the limo driver because he was with you, Dave."

"He still could've come up with the scheme," Joy noted.

"But again, we're still minus a motive," I said to her.

Vito said, "I think Joy and Dave and I have become superfluous to the Darby Coltrane part of the investigation, Captain Devereux. Hollywood Division is the right place for it to be handled, and you know everything we know. We should head back to Pittsburgh and work that end of things under Sheriff Boyce. But we'll keep in close touch and share our findings because all these murders overlap."

"But it's still too much of a goddamned who done it," Captain Devereux griped. "I can't help it, I *hate* whodunnits," he added.

114

CHAPTER 21

Come Saturday, when she could've gone to the park or the swimming pool in South Park, just a few miles from Pittsburgh proper, Carla mustered all of her fortitude to go to confession at St. Agnes Church in Pleasant Hills. She hoped she wouldn't see anyone she knew and was glad this particular church wasn't in her and Derrick's neighborhood. She knew that Vito Martinelli, that ex-cop who was working the Lance Goldman murder case, lived in Pleasant Hills with his second wife, thus it was enemy territory. Derrick had told her that. He hated Vito and his bosom buddy, that holier than thou filmmaker David Cristi who had refused to cast Jennifer Hubbara in that hackneyed umpteenth sequel of his. Not to mention David's daughter Joy, who already thought she was a female Sherlock Holmes and always went around acting as if her shit didn't stink.

Carla parked her little Hyundai and warily entered the massively imposing Catholic church, almost afraid that the marble statues of Jesus and the Virgin Mary would step down from their pedestals and strike her dead. She tried telling herself that her Savior surely would not have condemned her to the extent that the parishioners would. Jesus said, "Let he who is without sin cast the first stone." He also bestowed forgiveness upon Mary Magdalene, who had been a prostitute. In fact that bestselling book, *The Da Vinci Code*, had put forth an argument that Jesus Christ and Mary Magdalene might have been lovers. These rationalizations helped Carla pity herself and entertain hope that if she confessed all of her sins she would be forgiven, no matter how bad they were. She hoped the priest wouldn't yell at her. She hoped he would give her a lenient penance, maybe ten Our Fathers and ten Hail Maries instead of making her do all the Stations of the Cross all by herself, kneeling at each station in turn, all twelve stations, including The Agony of Christ, where anybody who came into the church would see her and know that she was indeed one of the most horrible of sinners.

In her wretched state of mine, she desperately wanted to believe that both she and Jennifer wanted to renounce their sinful ways and that they might actually become close friends once their rehabilitations was further along. On the other hand, she didn't completely trust that Jennifer was going to show up.

But as the heavy ornate door of the sacred place went shut behind her, she was relieved when she spotted Jennifer kneeling in a pew, all by herself. Carla didn't care for Jennifer's boyfriend, Giorgio, and was glad he wasn't there. She worked her way toward Jennifer and knelt beside her, whispering, "Please don't let me interrupt your prayers."

Jennifer whispered back, "I already made my confession and I'm also done saying my penance. But I won't leave. I'll wait till you come out."

She meant out of the confessional. But the protocol of the sacrament demanded that one should offer prayers to Jesus before confessing to the priest.

"Who's in there?" Carla whispered.

"Father Domka."

"That's what I hoped," said Carla. "Everyone wants him. He's nice."

She stayed in the pew and remained kneeling while she asked for forgiveness in advance of her actual confession. Then she got up and warily entered her side of the cubicle, then knelt and closed the door. In semi-darkness, facing the screened aperture through which Father Domka could hear her but could not see her well enough to identify her, she said the prescribed introductory prayer:

"Bless me, Father, for I have sinned. It has been three years since my last confession."

"Three years?" the disembodied voice on the other side of the aperture said in dismay. "You have gone that long without being in a state of grace?"

"Y-yes, Father."

"And during that time, did you take communion without first going to confession."

"No, Father," she said, greatly relieved that she could at least be truthful about that.

"I'm glad to hear that. It would have been a sacrilege and had you died during that time, you would have gone straight to hell."

"I know, Father. But I was afraid to confess."

"What sin were you afraid to tell?"

"Uh...I've been having sex with one of my male cousins, Father."

"My God! That is one of the worst sins imaginable!'

"I...I...know, Father."

"Well, I don't want to hear the rest of your confession, my dear. Instead I am going to recommend that you just keep right on doing what makes you feel good. And screwing your cousin does make you feel pretty good, does it not?"

She was stunned to silence -- and suddenly scared. Scared out of her wits, in fact.

A mocking laugh brayed from the priest's side of the confessional, and she jumped up and pushed the door open on her side.

Then she pulled open the priest's door -- and as she did so she heard Jennifer laughing behind her back. But yet that wasn't the worst part.

Because the braying laugh was coming from Giorgio, who was sitting beside the dead priest, who had a large knife in his throat, which had released a bright bib of blood.

"Bless you, my child," said Giorgio. "For you are forgiven."

CHAPTER 22

Vito, Joy and I were on an airplane when Carla Baressi and Father Domka were found murdered in St. Agnes Church in Pleasant Hills. The priest had suffered a stab wound in his neck and Carla's abdomen was ripped open from her stomach to her chest and her throat had been slit for good measure. We didn't find any of this out till the plane touched down and we turned our cell phones back on. That's when Vito saw that he had gotten about a dozen calls from Sheriff Boyce, called him back and got hit with the awful news. We were stunned that in our absence more killings had taken place -- and not far from where we lived.

Joy opened her laptop, booting it up in the back of Vito's car as soon as we exited Valet Parking. By the time we got on the ramp toward the Fort Pitt Tunnels she had learned all the gory details that hadn't been withheld by the police, and she filled us in.

"Pretty sickening," I said, utterly dismayed.

Joy said, "At least we now have a pretty good notion of whose work it all is. Jenny Hubbara, Giorgio Luviano or both."

"Can't argue with that," said Vito. "But what about Derrick Hubbara? We know he has a motive, thanks to Ryan Grace."

"For all six killings?" I asked, because that didn't yet add up for me.

"At the very least for Darby Coltrane and the unlucky guy who was collateral damage. Darby was the one person we're aware of who knew Derrick and his daughter were probably sleeping in the same bed. That gives both of them a motive."

119

"Sure does," said Joy. "They wouldn't want the whole world to find out."

I said, "Now that the killers are back in our territory, we may be better situated for solving all the cases than either Sheriff Boyce or Captain Devereux are. If they don't go off killing people somewhere else now."

"Right, Dave," Vito agreed. "I want to tell Sheriff Boyce I'm going to use the authority he gave me to put Derrick Hubbara in the hot seat. Same goes for Jenny and Giorgio -- if we can find them and bring them in."

"For that we might need the sheriff's manpower," Joy said.

"We'll almost certainly need that kind of help," said Vito. "And I'd rather use it instead of any of us taking unnecessary risks. Keep that in mind when you're on your own one of these days, Joy."

I can't tell you how glad I was, for my daughter's sake, to hear him say that.

Thinking over all that we had learned, both here and in Los Angeles, I began to feel we might be making headway. Vito had once said that sometimes intuition took over after days and days of flailing against the elusive particulars of a case that seemed to be going nowhere. He said we shouldn't push those feelings aside but should take heart in them. Neither should we tell anyone about them or we might jinx ourselves.

Maybe we were almost at the bottom of things. To paraphrase Sherlock Holmes, once we had eliminated everything that could *not* be true, what remained must be the truth no matter how absurd or repulsive. Giorgio Luviano and Jennifer Hubbara were definitely our main suspects now, with Derrick Hubbara lurking somewhere in the loop. I asked myself if it might be possible that Lance Goldman was murdered for learning the kinds of things Darby Coleman had babbled to Ryan Grace. I had little doubt that Ryan had given an accurate account of what Darby had told him, but did it mean Darby was telling him the truth or making a story up for the purpose of seduction? In other words, if rich and famous Derrick Hubbara was engaging in a sexual taboo, it was okay for Darby and Ryan to also give in to their own urges.

If Derrick was as twisted as Darby's story made him out to be, he could be aware of why his daughter and her boyfriend were choosing their victims. He may not have conspired with Jenny and Giorgio, but if he had indulged in a lust for his daughter from the time she was a little girl, her conflicted feelings of love versus hate may have exploded into a murder spree. I hoped what we had been told about the two of them would turn out to be a fever dream, a drunken fantasy, a tool for seduction used on Ryan Grace by Darby Coltrane. I had never really liked Derrick Hubbara and would have fought hard against his chance to direct *Dealey Plaza* if it had gone forward under Lance Goldman. And now, should the worst we had been told about him turn out to be true, I would hate that someone so malignant had been even a very small part of my career. But I told myself, let the chips fall where they may, the truth couldn't remain hidden. It had to come out.

It was hard for me to feel a grain of pity or understanding for a grown man who could harbor sexual desire for a child. To me, men like that should be removed from society and kept in a cage. I couldn't help feeling even more vindictive when the case of a missing five-year-old girl had rocked the nation just three years ago.

A registered sex offender living in a trailer camp not far from her home succeeded in abducting her, keeping as his "plaything" for two weeks, then putting her in a hole and letting her hug her teddy bear while he shoveled dirt on top of her. In his HBO Special at that time, comedian Dennis Miller said, "You know, if you ever feel an urge to do things to a child, do the world a favor: Go out and buy yourself a .38

121

revolver. Load just one bullet. Take yourself out before you act on your stinking impulses."

I don't think I can say it any better than that.

CHAPTER 23

Sheriff Boyce got an anonymous phone call the day before he was heading to Pittsburgh. He didn't recognize the tipster's voice, but he said it may have been disguised by one of those cheap electronic devices that were sold at Wal-Mart.

"Put some pressure on Derrick Hubbara. The Luger belonged to him. It was part of his collection," the tipster mouthed indistinctly, and hung up before the call could be traced.

The sheriff phoned Vito about it and Vito told me and Joy that same day. We all knew it had been withheld from the media that a partially melted Luger had been found in the burnt-out limousine.

Vito told me that Sheriff Boyce didn't want me to be there for the face-to-face with Derrick because there was too much baggage between the two of us, so I took my wife Diane and Vito's wife Donna to a Pittsburgh Pirate game to take the heat off of me and Vito for not spending enough time with them in recent weeks. It was on a Sunday, and both women had the day off. They both worked in the women's dress department at Penney's. Donna was an attractive blonde, ten years younger than Vito, and Donna was letting her hair go gray but was still perky, in her early sixties. We drank beer and ate fries, peanuts and hotdogs, and got stuffed.

We all enjoyed the game even though our team lost to the Atlanta Braves, who were being pressured to change their name to something that wasn't considered pejorative to Native Americans. They were stubbornly fighting against any change, feeling that it would turn off too many of their fans, and claiming it was "another abusive example of wrong-headed political correctness." Whatever duress it was causing them did not affect their ability to rack up singles,

doubles and homers, which made the game go on pretty long before we got to the seventh-inning stretch.

When we sat back down, losing seven to nothing, I made a further attempt to mollify the two wives by telling them, "Vito and Joy and I are planning a big picnic for when we solve the murder cases."

"How soon will that be?" Donna asked skeptically.

I said, "It's really coming together now. I can feel it."

"I hope so," she said. "I'm scared you're all in danger."

"So am I," Diane said. "Everyone who got killed is someone you know, Dave. I don't think you have any idea who's next."

My mind flashed to a spooky image of my daughter going up the front steps to Derrick Hubbara's house, and I comforted myself with the realization that she was with two armed men. I didn't think Derrick would try to pull anything on them, but what about Jenny and Giorgio, if they were the killers we were after? We didn't know where they were so we had no idea where they might be lurking.

"Joy almost got killed once before," Diane reminded me. Unnecessarily. Because the danger she might be under was never far from my thoughts. When the killer of my boyhood friend, Ron Demick, was about to be unmasked, he sent one of his minions to butcher Joy with a machete. It was sheer luck that Vito and I had stopped him.

I admitted to myself that Donna and Diane's worries weren't unfounded. By now, we had little doubt that Jenny Hubbara and Giorgio Luviano were our perpetrators. Since we hadn't zeroed in on a motive for their string of murders we couldn't be sure who they might go after next, but we understood that murder was often self-perpetuating. Even if it started out with a sense of logic such as a quest for revenge, it could mutate into a blood lust devoid of purpose. I thought this might have happened to the killers we were dealing with. If so, the joy of killing was now their motive, and they were harboring a thirst for it that could never be appeased.

CHAPTER 24

As Vito and I were with Sheriff Boyce in his official county-supplied vehicle, we talked over the particulars we needed to have in mind for his interrogation of Derrick Hubbara. I didn't mind missing out on the Pirate game with my dad, my stepmother and Vito's wife because I was glad to be on this escapade and very excited.

Unknown to Derrick, he had been under surveillance by a rotating team of the sheriff's men for the past week or so and two members of the team were being kept on standby today, somewhere down the block. Derrick didn't know the sheriff was about to barge in on him. He hadn't been notified because Sheriff Boyce wanted to take him by surprise. In case he refused to open the front door, the two members of the surveillance team on standby were equipped with riot guns and a battering ram.

We believed Derrick was probably unaware that we knew about the convention money that was stolen from his safe and the tip the sheriff had gotten that he had once owned a Luger which could have been the very one used to kill Lance Goldman and his driver. We would have the element of surprise regarding both those issues. When we talked them over on our way to Derrick's house in a gentrified section of Pittsburgh, we all thought it likely that either Giorgio Luviano or Jenny Hubbara had phoned the tip in and that they had also stolen the cash. We had a theory that Derrick might actually know where they happened to be right now, whereas we still had no clue. We also agreed among the three of us that Sheriff

Boyce would be the lead interrogator, not only because he insisted upon it but because Derrick harbored a contempt for me, my dad and Vito that might make him inclined to blow us off.

We hoped he wouldn't just ask for his attorney right off the bat.

Sheriff Boyce didn't hammer as hard as he could on the oaken door but just pushed a button and we faintly heard a bell ringing somewhere inside the refurbished three-story hundred-year-old house. It dated back to the Reconstruction period after the Civil War and would've been considered a mansion back then. I would've liked living there except I would not have loved the task of dusting all the heavy Victorian furniture it likely had back then; that would have required a maid.

Sheriff Boyce pushed doorbell a couple more times, then Derrick Hubbara opened the door. He was wearing jeans and a sweat-soaked T-shirt bearing an image of himself in one of his movie roles, and he was wiping the sweat beads from his face with a large white towel. He seemed startled when he saw the sheriff's uniform but he recovered quickly. "Sorry, I was working out in my weight room. Sheriff Boyce, right? I'm bad with names."

"Well, you got mine right," said the sheriff. "Detective Martinelli and his colleague Joy Cristi are with me as well."

"Well, come in. Is there bad news?" he asked uneasily. "Something had to bring all three of you to my house."

"Something surely did," said the sheriff, "and by and by I'll let you know the details. Show us to where we can sit and talk. Are you alone right now?"

"Yes, my daughter is off somewhere. Let's go into my screening room. It has comfortable theater-style seats."

"What about the dining room?" I asked him. "Maybe we can sit around the table and I'd have room for my laptop."

"Certainly, let's go there," he agreed.

The hallway that led to the living room and the living room itself were filled with large movie posters, the kind used in theaters, called one-sheets. There must have been around twenty of them, expensively framed, not in the cheap poster frames sold at Wal-Mart. All the artwork was from Hubbara's movies, nobody else's. Action hero Blaze Stewart, the machinegun-toting flame-throwing character he had made famous, was featured in all his menacing muscle-flexing undefeatable glory in every poster. But that was fiction. We knew that in real life he had vulnerabilities like everyone else, like the rest of struggling humanity in other words, and we were hoping to knock him off of his game.

As we seated ourselves around his glass-topped coffee table, he said, "I can show all of you around upstairs, after we're done talking. I've made it into a mini-museum up there and I like to show it off."

"Let's see how things go first," Sheriff Boyce told him. "Do you and your daughter each have bedrooms up there?"

It was said off-handedly but it obviously shook Derrick up.

He blinked, folded his hands, squirmed a little and sat back. Then he said, "Hers is part of the museum now. I needed the space and she's gone a lot."

"Where does she sleep when she's here?" the sheriff persisted.

"Well...she doesn't mind sleeping on the couch in one of the museum rooms. It has a pull-out bed for guests." He got lost in thought for a moment, then said, "I may have to clear out another room and let her use it now that *Zombie Kidz* is on hiatus."

"That all seems a little odd to me," said the sheriff.

Derrick managed a chuckle of the sort learned in acting class-- at least that's what it sounded like to me. Something to get him past the moment. I glanced at Vito to see if he picked up on it, but kept taking notes on my laptop.

Derrick said, "I can't deny us showbiz people can be sort of odd, Sheriff. Eccentricity is almost a part of the Hollywood game."

"How much do you worry about Jennifer when she's not here?" Sheriff Boyce asked.

"Well, she has a chaperone when she travels. The studio provides it. And when she's here she has me. I take good care of her even though she thinks she's more grown-up than she really is. At least she's not suing me for her independence like some other young actresses do. I hope it never happens. I've always tried not to spoil her."

As he said all that, we let him ramble. But we weren't inclined to believe he was such a caring and responsible father instead of just the opposite.

"Jeez!" he said, pushing back from the table. "I forgot to offer you guys anything. I have a refrigerator full of health drinks. You name it I probably have it. I also have Orange juice, grape juice and Gatorade. Or I can make coffee if you need the caffeine."

"I'll take Gatorade," Vito said, and the sheriff and I opted for grape juice. Derrick got up to fetch it, and we were glad to have him out of the room for a while so we could compare our thoughts.

Sheriff Boyce said to me and Vito, in a low whisper, "He got touchy and stayed that way when I asked about his daughter."

Vito agreed, saying, "Keep on it. Keep him rattled and we'll see what comes out of him."

I said, "I don't think we'll get much more. He's going to get more reticent."

When Derrick returned with our drinks on a tray and was handing them out, Sheriff Boyce said, "I know that you were used to keeping a large amount of cash in your safe, and somebody got hold of the combination and stole it all. Who do you think did that?"

"Who told you that, some blabbermouth?" Derrick said as he sat back down. "I don't know who did it, but it wasn't my daughter if that's what you're thinking."

"I think I'd have to suspect her if I were you," Sheriff Boyce said.

"I...I don't think she would do that," Derrick muttered. His face got sweaty again and he used a napkin to wipe it.

"Why not?" Sheriff Boyce said. "You indicated how anxious she is to grow up and be on her own, and the money would certainly help her do that."

"My daughter isn't a thief!" Derrick said indignantly.

"We've heard some strange things about you and her," Vito interjected with a sly look on his face.

"It's only hearsay and we don't know what to think of it," Sheriff Boyce said. "Do you have any idea what people are referring to?"

"Not a clue. Strange goings on? What the hell are they talking about?"

"Your relationship with Jenny is totally above board and always has been?" the sheriff asked.

"Who the hell has said otherwise?" Derrick angrily demanded.

Sheriff Boyce didn't directly answer that but pretended to mull over his next question. Then he said, "Back to the robbery of your safe, I suggest we dust it for fingerprints. You don't want to think ill of your daughter, which is perfectly understandable. But from our standpoint we must consider that she lived here with you and must've seen you open and close the safe many times. She also had access to your weapons collection. Do you keep it under lock and key?"

130

"Definitely," Derrick staunchly responded. "I'm anal retentive about my guns. Nobody touches them but me. Absolutely nobody."

"Do you own a German Luger?"

"No. But I'd buy one probably, if somebody showed one to me."

"May we have a look at your weapons? Just to see how you keep other people from getting their hands on them."

"Absolutely. They're on display in one of the larger rooms upstairs on the third floor. My mini museum occupies most of the second floor other than my bedroom, bathroom and dressing room suite."

He got up and so did we, and followed him up the first flight of stairs, and on the landing, he said, "Want a sneak peek?"

Looking past him through a set of double doors, I could see there was some kind of furry monster in there. I almost jumped and Derrick laughed when he saw te look on my face, but Vito and Sheriff Boyce made n audible reaction.

"That's Johnny," Derrick said. "He's vicious but he won't hurt you here, only in the movies. I named him after Jack Nicholson in *The Shining*. Don't be scared. Come on."

"I was a bit startled but not really scared," I said. "I'm not a namby-pamby person."

He said, "I didn't think you were."

"We don't want to fool around too much," said Sheriff Boyce. "Let's just take a quick look and move on. To the upstairs."

Derrick led us into what he had called his mini-museum and Vito, the sheriff and I went from here to there, looking at whatever we chose, but not for long because none of it was uppermost in our minds. I remember seeing displays of bloody arms and legs, a decapitated body and a bloody head in a basket beneath a huge bloody blade encased in an arrangement of timber and rope.

"Is that a real guillotine?" I asked.

"Sure is," Derrick said proudly. "It used to be in Kennywood Park, and I bought it from them. They made me pay a steep price when they found out who I am. But it was one of my favorite things when our school picnics were held there every year, so I felt like I had to have it."

"Let's go," Sheriff Boyce said brusquely. "Take us to your weapon collection."

We climbed the second flight of stairs and entered a twenty by fifteen room that Derrick had to unlock. That's where he had a panoramic display of many kinds of tools for mayhem, all in glass cases against the walls.

"Impressive," said the sheriff. "Not as vast as the collection the FBI has, but impressive nonetheless."

Vito was already moving from glass case to glass case, each with the kind of glass doors that bore little steel locks.

I said to Derrick, "Between all the props you have in your museum and all the items in here, it must add up to a fortune. What if it was all lost in a fire? Do you have insurance?"

He smiled self-assuredly and said, "Through Wells Fargo. Five million dollars. I had to go high since so much of it was used in my movies and that elevates their worth sky-high in the eyes of serious collectors."

Vito said, "I don't see a Luger in this case of about forty handguns," Vito said.

"Neither do I," said Sheriff Boyce, who was standing beside Vito.

"I told you I don't *have* a Luger," Derrick shot back at them.

"Well, then, I've seen enough," the sheriff said. "Don't leave town without letting us know, Derrick. Other questions may come up."

"I'll do anything I can to help," Derrick responded, the picture of cooperation.

We went back down the two staircases and took our leave of him. As soon as we got into the sheriff's vehicle, Vito asked, "Are you gonna drop the surveillance?"

"Hell no, I don't trust the sly bastard."

"You think he had a Luger at some point prior to the murders?" I asked.

"I still think it's entirely possible."

"I think I can find out for sure," I said. "He told me he's insured through Wells Fargo."

We discussed key aspects of the interview as the sheriff drove to Clairton to drop me and Vito off at Vito's office, and on the way we decided to detour to a bar and restaurant called the Terrace Garden, where there was barbecue on Sundays. "You're gonna like it," Vito told Sheriff Boyce.

"I believe you 'cause you're a man who likes to eat," the sheriff acknowledged.

"Don't let Joy's petite look fool you," Vito said. "She works hard to maintain it, but she's a trencher woman when she wants to be."

"I want to be right now," I said. "I really like their barbecued ribs."

When we got to the Terrace Garden the bar was packed so we sat in the dining room, at a corner table apart from the others, to avoid any possible eavesdroppers. After we ordered our food and got our drinks and started in on a round of beers, we discussed the things we had lately learned and how it all fit in with our investigation. When our food arrived, we switched to talking about more pleasant things and laid the grislier things aside. But when I got home, I typed up a summation:

(1) We can't dismiss Darby Coltrane's implication, as revealed to Ryan Grace, that Derrick Hubbara is or was molesting his daughter.

(2) It seems possible, and perhaps probable, as was told by Gary Chelton to David Cristi, that Derrick was having sex with his niece, Carla Baressi, up until the day she was murdered.

(3) It is likely that Jennifer Hubbara, perhaps in cahoots with her boyfriend, Giorgio Luviano, stole a large amount of money from Derrick's safe.

(4) Jennifer and Giorgio may be our killers and Derrick may or may not be fully aware of it.

(5) Derrick may have owned a Luger at one time and it may be the weapon used in the murders of Lance Goldman and his limo driver.

(6) Tracking down Jennifer and Giorgio is a top priority.

I emailed copies of my report to Vito, Sheriff Boyce and my dad. Then I sat in front of my TV with it tuned to a true-crime show while my brain was occupied with details of our own murder cases and the gist of the show on TV didn't sink in.

Before I went to Vito's office the next morning, I phoned Sheriff Boyce and asked him to send me the passenger lists for flights from LAX into Pittsburgh in or around the day of Lance Goldman's murder. He said that he would, and he understood why I was asking and he'd be looking forward to whatever I found out. Then I said, "I wonder if you could subpoena Derrick Hubbara's Wells Fargo insurance policy on his weapons collection."

And he said, "I catch your drift, Joy. I think I can do that, too."

CHAPTER 25

Jennifer Hubbara knew Giorgio Luviano as well as she knew the back of her own hand, and she also knew, quite smugly, that she held him in the palm of it. She was precociously wise to the desires of men and the blandishments of sex, and she sized him up and thought to herself he would do, when she first laid eyes on him on the set of *Zombie Hunterz*. He had come there as part of a tour group hosted by Jose Della Cruz, the very man whom her father beat up not long afterwards. Jennifer smirked behind Giorgio's back at his perpetual sneer and impudent attitude, and right away she pegged him as a small man with a giant-sized inferiority complex and felt she could control him and bend him to her wishes.

It turned out he was an easy conquest. He became so infatuated with her, so totally smitten it was as if he had never had sex before and wasn't at all aware that he couldn't satisfy her. It wasn't hard to make him do anything she wanted him to do. She was dominant and he was subservient, and if he had any awareness of the true nature of their relationship, he never complained, never even mentioned it. She almost had to laugh at him. He was in complete thrall, lost in the fantasies she created for him and perpetuated. She had him utterly believing that if they could escape with all the cash they had stolen from her father they would live happily ever after as man and wife. He thought she was with him all the way on that even though it was never one of her intentions.

She liked to get him talking about himself so he would reveal his sins, his weaknesses, his inner demons, his sick, poorly planned crimes. Sex was a handy device to wheedle it all out of him. The crimes he had committed were vicious but pathetic. She learned he had been manipulated and led into them by his own brother, exactly the way she was manipulating him now. He and Dominic had been abandoned at birth and were abused sexually in an orphanage until they were adopted at ages eight and ten by a middle-aged couple who abused them in other ways. Their adoptive parents, Barney and Helga Schultz, owned a rugged farm in West Virginia with boulders and tree stumps sticking up all over the sixty-five acres.

So guess who had to chop, burn or dig up the tree stumps and haul the boulders away in a wheel barrow? Of course, the two orphan boys. They were adopted to be kept isolated and enslaved by Barney and Helga, who needed cheap labor to save them from bankruptcy. They constantly threatened to send Giorgio and Dominic back to the orphanage if they didn't do exactly what they were told. The two boys were beaten with the buckle end of a leather strap as punishment for misbehavior or for being sinful or lazy. They were made to wear long-sleeved garments and full-length trousers to hide welts, bruises and bloody scabs when the boys went to school. But as miserable as their life on the farm was, they dreaded to be sent back to the orphanage where the kind of abuse put on them made them doubt who they were in terms of gender or sexual preference. They despised queers and didn't want to be that way, but they were forced to perform those kinds of acts.

"We don't have to keep you," Mr. and Mrs. Schultz would say. "We didn't sign any papers. They'll take you back if we ask them to."

In the parlor the boys' adoptive parents had put up a portrait of Adolf Hitler that they hid when Child Protective Services showed up every once in a while, and the boys had to be issued

136

a severe warning. "Keep your damn mouths shut till they're gone. You'll be sorry if you're not nice and pleasant while they're here. We'll make sure you're *good* and sorry after they leave. They'll take you if we ask them to."

Barney and Helga were closeted neo-Nazi sympathizers. They received Nazi literature in the mail and hid it in the piano bench, under its hinged lid, with sheet music piled on top in case anyone from CPS got too curious.

As they got older the two adopted brothers read the propaganda more than Helga and Barney did. By the time they reached adolescence they started to think of themselves as part of the White Resistance, anxious to grow up and be staunchly active in The Movement. As they absorbed racist doctrines they became imbued with a raging inner hatred of their captors, their slave masters, which in the truest sense their adoptive "parents" actually were.

When Dominick was eighteen and Giorgio was sixteen, the older brother was bold enough to say to the younger one, "Why don't we just kill them and hide their bodies? Then we can just live here by ourselves and do what we want. They must be hiding money somewhere. We can say they abandoned us and we don't know where they are."

It scared Giorgio to think that way at first. But little by little his brother persuaded him. And one night, lying in the one sagging bed that they both shared, Giorgio whispered, "Where would we hide their bodies so the cops wouldn't find them?"

"At first I thought, in the well," Dominic said. "But what if they bunched up, one on top of the other, and didn't go all the way down?"

That made the boys giggle.

Giorgio said, "The cops would come because they would start to stink."

And they both giggled again.

"What would we use to kill them with?" Giorgio said. "I wouldn't trust that old shotgun Barney has in the garage. It might blow up on us. I never even seen him shoot it."

"What've we been usin' to chop stumps?" Dominic asked rhetorically.

They both then knew they would use the axes. They didn't have to say it out loud. They just knew it.

That still left the issue of what to do with their victims' corpses. But finally Dominic came up with the answer. "Neither of us has a driver license 'cause they wouldn't let us, but we both been drivin' that ol' tractor a lot. And it has a cart we can hitch to it. I think we should dig a big hole in advance and have it ready. Then after we do it to 'em we put 'em both in the cart and take 'em to the grave we already dug, maybe put creosote or lime on top of 'em afore we cover 'em up."

Giorgio said, "That might work, and we might not get caught if we take 'em deep enough and far enough back where the woods are thick."

"Not too thick. We need an open enough place to dig," Dominic said.

And they both giggled again.

Dominic grew quiet and thought for a while. Then he said, "Why should we have to hunt for their stash? Why don't we torture the hell out of 'em both? They deserve it. We can make 'em tell us where the money's hid instead of havin' to bust our asses searchin'."

"Now you're talkin'," Giorgio said, lying there in the dark.

Eight days later, after the grave was secretly dug, they butchered Barney and Helga, not in the house or barn where they would have to work hard to clean up the bloody mess, but out in a field where they could shovel dirt and cover up the evidence. Then they hauled them in the cart behind the tractor to bury them in the pre-chosen spot.

To their surprise, for several weeks no one came around looking for Barney or Helga. The old farmers so seldom went into town that they weren't missed. Not only that but they had always kept to themselves. They didn't linger in the stores or taverns. They bought the things they needed and went directly home.

"Now they'll always be home," Dominic joked.

"Home sweet home like that doily she crocheted," Giorgio said.

They laughed pretty hard.

They had split around fifteen thousand dollars that used to belong to their adoptive parents, so they both applied for driver licenses and practiced driving Barney's battered pickup truck around the fields till they dared to take it onto a couple of the dirt roads for a lot more practice. Then they both took their driving tests and Giorgio passed on his first try but it took Dominic two tries.

One day when they rode into town they were able to buy a rifle and pistol each. This made them feel great. Their urge to do something patriotic for the White Struggle built up in them all the more since they could now read the pamphlets that came in the mail on the porch or in the kitchen or living room with nobody to tell them not to.

On another of their trips to town they saw two wimpy guys with their arms around each other being heckled by three tough, angry guys outside one of the bars. They were calling the wimpy-looking guys faggots and such and grabbing their crotches and saying, "I got somethin' fer ya, ya fuckin' queers!"

Giorgio and Dominic watched and wanted to join in. At least Giorgio did, but Dominic pulled him back.

"What's the matter? Let's go get 'em!" Giorgio said.

"We do that we'll turn ourselves into suspects."

"Huh? Suspects for what? They're *homos!*"

"Right. So we're gonna kill 'em," Dominic muttered slyly. "And when we do we don't wanna have the cops botherin' us, do we? We just want 'em to think we don't pick on nobody, we just always stay out of it and mind our own bidness."

"Makes sense," said Giorgio.

It took them a couple weeks to find out all they could about the two homosexuals, what their names were, where they worked and where they lived, which was in a nice little house with flowers in the yard, not far from town.

"Fuckin' fags *would* have flowers!" Dominic scoffed one day when they drove by slowly in the pickup, casing the place. Two nights later they broke in by smashing a pane of glass in the back door. The two lovers were awakened by the noise and they jumped up as Dominic and Giorgio burst into their bedroom and started blasting away with their pistols. One of them didn't die right away and had to be shot a couple more times. Giorgio got blood spatter on his face and on his lips and in his open mouth, which made him gag when he swallowed it, breathing hard, as he and Dominic ran from the bedroom, leaving it a bloody mess, and jumped into their pickup truck and peeled out.

They laid low for several weeks, according to their plan. But just as when they killed Barney and Helga, once again nothing happened. No cops showed up pounding on their front door. No battering ram, no posse, no tear gas, no bloodhounds trying to sniff out a couple of dead bodies. Their fear and apprehension of all that wore off and they eventually forgot to talk about it. Instead, they began making other plans.

"In case they ever do come after us, it might be better if we split up for a while," Dominic said one day. "I'm thinkin' I'd like to head toward someplace where it's nice and warm all the time, like Florida. I'm thinkin' to drive that miserable old pickup till it craps out, then hitchhike the rest of the way down to Miami. Maybe git some kinda job down there, I don't care what."

"That's funny," said Giorgio. "I'd like to be somewhere I never been before, like you, only I'd head the other way, like to California. Los Angeles. Charles Manson made a big name for his self in San Francisco, only he got caught. I don't want that. I'd keep a low profile out there, just like here, but with the cash we split up I'd maybe take acting lessons or crew lessons, somethin' like that maybe."

Dominic laughed and said, "Hey, I can see you got stars in yer eyes, bro!"

"You always told me to think big, Dominic."

"So I did, so I did, bro."

CHAPTER 26

Following up on Joy's suggestion, Sheriff Boyce closely examined a sheaf of flight records till he came across what he had half expected to find once she had prompted him. He felt a glow of satisfaction that he would gladly share with Joy when he saw that Jennifer Hubbara and Giorgio Luviano had flown from LAX into Pittsburgh International Airport two days prior to the murders of Lance Goldman and his limo driver.

He was about to break the news to Vito and Joy on a conference call when the desk sergeant handed him a package from Fedex. He couldn't wait to open it because he knew it would contain his subpoenaed copy of Derrick Hubbara's Wells Fargo insurance policy on his weapon collection. He immediately rifled through the document till he came across photos and valuations of each weapon, and to his delight there were two full-frame photos of a German Luger plus a close-up of its serial number. It was insured for four thousand seven hundred dollars.

Now he leapt at the chance to make that conference call. As soon as Vito and Joy were looped in, he thanked her for prompting him and filled them both in.

"Wow!" Vito said. "Four grand and then some is a high valuation. He was fixing to rip off his insurance company if he ever filed a claim. I used to have one and I only got sixteen hundred for it. Some of them go for a lot more. If you had one owned by Hitler or Goering and you could prove it, it'd probably be worth over a million bucks."

"Next time I'm in your end of the woods, I owe you both a steak dinner. This calls for a toast. Joy gets the credit though."

"Thanks," Joy said. "I'll look forward to it."

Sheriff Boyce said, "Even though Jennifer and Giorgio landed at the airport only a couple days before the first two murders were committed, it still doesn't nail them as our perpetrators. They were in the right place at the right time but to move forward to a prosecution we would need more evidence. Also, the fact that Derrick lied when he said he never owned a Luger does not prove that the one he did own was the murder weapon. We weren't able to the serial number on the half melted Luger found n the ashes of the limo. Forensics can't say for certain it was the one Derrick Hubbara insured some time ago."

"I still think it was his," Vito said. "It's too much of a coincidence. If it walks like a duck and talks like a duck it's a duck, guys."

He meant we were still lacking one of the three M's that were the hallmark of all murder investigations. We could now show that Jennifer and Giorgio had Means and Opportunity. But what was their Motive?

I decided I had to confide the gossipy, unverified things I was told at the Pittsburgh Horror Convention by Gary Chelton and Leona Hubbara. "Leona is Derrick's ex-wife and Gary is a big blustery guy who lets it fly even when he shouldn't. Leona babbled about Derrick supposedly parading naked around Jenny when she was five years old, and Gary thinks Derrick was having an affair with his cousin Carla, the young lady who was murdered at St. Agnes with Father Domka. What if Jennifer was jealous of Carla? And what if she's harboring a grudge against men, particularly child molesters? But one thing that sticks in my craw is that we haven't come up with any evidence that Lance Goldman ever sexually abused anyone, so why did somebody want him dead?"

143

"Maybe because he knew something about Derrick," Vito conjectured. "But when Mr. Action Hero was told that the murder weapon was a Luger he appeared not to have known it till then. He looked stunned."

"And it didn't come off like an act," Sheriff Boyce said.

I said, "He's not a good actor, but he's not stupid, and he to know why you asked him if he owned a Luger because it was as good as telling him it was the kind of gun used."

"It would have been a short leap," said Vito, "for him to realize that his daughter or her boyfriend must've stolen his gun, which would tell him they were the killers. And if he put two and two together to that extent, he might also know why they did it."

"But he won't tell us because he doesn't want to rat out his daughter," Joy said.

"I'll put him in the hot seat and sweat it out of him," Sheriff Boyce said. "Meantime I'll put out a BOLO on Jennifer and Giorgio. Maybe if they have to hole up somewhere they won't be able to kill anybody else for a while."

"What about Derrick?" Vito said. "What is he likely to do next? Would he kill his daughter to save his own ass?"

I said, "Derrick is a totally self-centered malignant narcissist who flies by the seat of his pants. He gives in to his urges, does what he wants to do without thinking about consequences, and trusts that it will turn out okay. And when it doesn't he makes somebody else pay."

"Then unintended consequences are going to be his downfall," Vito said. "You can quote me on that.

CHAPTER 27

We decided that Vito and would I go with Sheriff Boyce to confront Derrick Hubbara with our discovery that he had once owned a German Luger and had lied about it. We were armed with the ammunition we needed in order to rattle him into admitting whatever he knew or suspected about his daughter and her boyfriend, including their potential involvement in a of murders. Meantime, Joy had traced Giorgio Luviano's whereabouts back to the days when he and his older brother, Dominic, were removed from an orphanage to a farm in West Virginia, from which they had apparently absconded after their adoptive parents disappeared. Law enforcement suspected they had been murdered. Neither they nor their remains had ever been found.

Joy came to my house at nine o'clock in the morning to drop off a copy of her latest summary of our findings on the interlocking murder cases, then she left for West Virginia by herself, pooh-poohing my tendency to worry about her and my advice that she should team up with one of Sheriff Boyce's deputies . "You might be heading into a hornet's nest of some kind," I warned her. "Who knows what went on down there?"

"Yes, Daddy, I know *Deliverance* was one of your favorite movies," she mocked me.

"I liked the banjo duet, not the movie so much," I said. "Although ironically it dealt with deviant rape, which is what *we're* dealing with too."

She didn't say anything to that. She just grimaced, got into her car and drove away.

A half hour later, Sheriff Boyce pulled his official department vehicle into my driveway with Vito in the passenger seat, and Vito pulled the back rest forward so I could climb in back. This time Derrick Hubbara had been told in advance that we were coming because we wanted him to be on edge. We believed he would be smart enough not to panic and run no matter the extent of his guilt in any of the matters on our agenda.

During the half-hour drive, we discussed matters pertaining to what we were about to do, and within about half an hour we pulled up in front of Hubbara's gentrified urban home. But when we stepped onto his porch and Sheriff Boyce pushed the bell button a number of times, he failed to come to the door.

"I'll get him on his cell phone," the sheriff said, "and if he knows what's good for him he damned well better answer."

But he didn't.

Like three prowlers, we sort of meandered around the side of the house and into the backyard, where there was a flagstone patio and some sliding glass doors -- and the doors were open.

"Some sense of security the dumbass has," Sheriff Boyce said as he let himself in and Vito and I followed.

"Wellness check?' Vito whispered, ascertaining that was the excuse Boyce would use for going in without a warrant, and the sheriff nodded.

Again feeling like burglars, led by Sheriff Boyce, we prowled from the kitchen through the dining room and into the living room and saw and heard nothing, but at least Vito and the sheriff were familiar with the layout due to their previous visit.

"Upstairs or downstairs?" Vito whispered.

"Try that cellar door," the sheriff responded.

Vito pulled the door open and we heard classical music coming from the basement.

"Maybe he's exercising down there. That's likely where he does it," Vito said.

The sheriff said nothing. He hesitated only slightly before leading the way down the basement steps, which were untypical in the sense that they had been thickly carpeted in red.

When we got to the bottom of the steps the first thing noticed was the lower half of Derrick's body lying supine on an exercise bench. But he wasn't whooshing and pushing against the heavy barbell that had been lowered from its rack.

It was the kind of rack with a ratchet that would prevent the bar from crashing down on him if he failed to make one of his reps and needed to get out from underneath.

But that feature of the rack hadn't been in use, or had been disengaged. The heavily loaded barbell was all the way down, pressing hard across Derrick's throat. His face was pasty white, his neck was crusted with dried blood and his larynx was crushed. His pectorals still were huge, but oddly flaccid in death.

"I guess he who lives by the barbell dies by the barbell," Vito quipped in his sardonically irreverent way.

None of us laughed.

It was gallows humor, a habit of Vito's that needed no fanfare or applause, which only would've encouraged him.

CHAPTER 28

I never listened to news on the radio in my car while I was traveling but much preferred listening to CD's by some of my favorite entertainers. I selected one by Sinatra, one by Sammy Davis and one by Mel Torme and laid them on the passenger seat so they'd be handy. Then I inserted the Torme disc and hit the gas pedal. The three CD's had a total running time of an hour and fifteen minutes which would closely coincide with my anticipated driving time.

I had researched the town of Hundred, West Virginia, where Giorgio and Dominic Luviano had gone to grade school and high school. The rugged old farm where they had lived after being adopted was twelve miles from Hundred, population only 307. I wondered how it could maintain any kind of school system, and I figured it must draw on children not just from Hundred but also from all the surrounding areas. The combined elementary and middle school was called Long Drain School and the high school was Hundred High School. I passed both school before I got on the main drag.

According to my notes, the town was named after Henry "Old Hundred" Church who died in 1860 at the age of 109. His wife Hannah also was a centenarian. He was a soldier in the British Army under General Cornwallis and was captured by American troops under General LaFayette. Echoes of true American history right there in a nutshell. When he was freed at the end of the Revolutionary War, he bought land enough to build a cabin with his own hands, on Fish Creek. He paid for the land with the musket he had carried before he got captured.

As a history buff, like my dad, I was charmed by those kinds of tidbits. The town was less than two hours from Pittsburgh via US 79 and State Route 18 and when I got there, I parked on the main street and walked around enjoying its quaint and charming aspect. It had a community swimming pool, a playground and pavilion, a town library and an impressive new fire station. Also, an old-fashioned general store, a pizza parlor, a second-hand book store, and an eatery famous for its homemade pies, which I hoped to partake of if I got a chance to have lunch.

I took a moment to linger in front of Miss Blue's Old Time Family Restaurant and read the chalkboard in the plate-glass window featuring amazingly low prices for specialties like peanut butter cake and cherry, apple and butterscotch pie. I decided to go in and see if I could start a conversation with somebody swho could help me achieve my mission down here, which was to learn as much as I could about Giorgio Luviano's young life before he left for California. What better way to do that than to find a local somebody familiar with local lore? If I didn't totally get what I wanted from a person or two in the restaurant, next I would try cornering a librarian or maybe a teacher, which might not be possible because the schools were closed for the summer.

Butterscotch pie was my ultimate favorite in the whole wide world, but I could hardly ever find a place that made it, therefore it was calling out to me even more than the peanut butter cake was. So, I yielded to temptation and went in. One of the things I loved best about being a private investigator, even though she didn't have my license yet, was that it wasn't a nine to five job. I got to travel, meet unusual people and see a lot of strange places without punching a clock. I liked being in this little town quaintly called Hundred even though the murder cases never strayed far from my mind even on this lovely July day which made me feel as if I had stepped through a time gap

149

into a semi-forgotten era. It might've been a quite pleasant deja vu sif it wasn't coupled with a spooky feeling of walking in the footsteps of a person who had his origins here and somehow had turned himself into a killer.

Miss Blue's Old Time Family Restaurant was air conditioned and had white walls with blue trim, which displayed lots of brightly colored happy-looking prints of idyllic Life on the Farm Days Gone By. The glass counters were sparkling clean and full of delicious looking cakes, pies and pastries. The wooden tables each had four bentwood chairs and were adorned with woven earthen placemats and green metal holders containing salt and pepper; ketchup and mustard; sugar and artificial sweetener; napkins and big laminated menus.

What a nice place to be in, I thought to myself as I was told by a chubby thirty-something waitress to take any table I wanted. She was wearing an overly starched white dress and blouse and an apron with carrots, tomatoes and onions silk-screened onto it, and she followed me to the corner table I chose and asked me if I wanted coffee. "Yes, cream and sugar, please," I told her, and she smiled and pleasantly said, "Sugar's right there, young miss. I'll be back in a jiffy to pour you some coffee for you. Regular, not decaff. You're sure to find somethin' you'd like on our new menu. Never seen you in here before, I don't think. Call me Sherry."

I could tell Sherrywas prompting me for information about myself, so I said, "I've never been here before, but it seems like a wonderful place to call home."

"Plannin' on stayin'?" she immediately probed.

"No, but maybe I'll come back for another visit sometime."

Three men in bibbed coveralls and plaid shirts at one of the other tables, eating with their grease-stained baseball caps on their heads, seemed to perk up and listen.

150

It dawned on me that the town was so small that if just one new person chose to take up residence, it would increase the population of 307 by one-third of a percent. Mark Twain had said his birth in the tiny hamlet of Hannibal, Missouri, that had increased its population of 100 by one percent without much giving him a whole lot of bother doing it, thus it proved he could've done as much for any town in America, if he had wanted to.

"I'm actually trying to find information on some people I used to know," I said off-handedly to Sherry. "A man and wife, the Schultz's, who worked a farm close by, adopted a couple of boys from an orphanage some few years back."

"My gosh! Everybody in this here town knows about *them!*" Sherry exclaimed loudly, causing the other patrons to turn their heads. "The boys ran away or were kidnapped," she went on, "and the good lord only knows whatever was done to Barney and Helga. If they was killed, their bodies ain't never been found. And some folks say the two young boys was..." She lowered her voice to a whisper. "...prostituted."

"No, that's not true," I said. "I happen to know one of them, the one whose name is Giorgio. He may have committed a crime up north. That's why I'm hoping to find him. Has he been seen around here lately? He might be traveling with a pretty young girl."

Sherry looked shocked and puzzled for a long moment, but finally she said, "If anything that creepy ever happened around here, ever'one woulda knowed and would still be talkin' about it. *Nothing* ever happens around here anymore, not since the whole Schultz family up and disappeared. Gosh! I better fetch your coffee."

"Wait, I said. "I already know what I want to try. "How much would it cost for a half serving of your peanut butter cake and a half serving of butterscotch pie on the same plate?"

"Same as a full order of either one of 'em. We ain't fussy around here. We try our best to do what the customer wants."

Within a few minutes, my lovely desserts were brought to me, and my coffee was poured. Sherry looked preoccupied while she was doing it. Then she said, "I been thinkin'. You'd do yourself good if you went and talked to our librarian, Mildred Jefferson. She teaches English at the high school in the fall and winter, and both those missing boys was students of hers. The library is her summer job."

This made me anxious to finish my wondrously delicious pie and cake, but I made myself go slow and fully enjoy it with a coffee refill along the way. My tab was only eight dollars, so I left and ten and two ones on the placemat under my empty plate -- a fifty percent tip to make Sherry happy. She unknowingly deserved it due to the information I had gotten from her.

CHAPTER 29

At first neither Vito nor I were going to phone Joy to tell her we had found Derrick dead in his basement. She had plenty enough to handle down there and we didn't want to throw her off her game if we didn't have to.

I said, "Maybe she won't hear about it if she isn't near a television set."

Vito snorted. "They're in the sticks, not on another planet. The media outlets are all having a field day. Nobody who isn't deaf or blind can avoid the blather. Derrick has millions of fans everywhere -- especially the kids. They're the ones who line up to see his movies or even sleep on the sidewalk overnight if they have to. You of all people should know that, David."

"Yeah, of course I do, Vito. I just don't want to shake up my daughter."

He blinked disparagingly at me and said, "Let her be, she's a big gal. You don't need to be a mother hen."

"But what if Luviano is hiding out down there with Jennifer? Joy might be walking into a trap -- and they're armed to the teeth with her father's weapons, for chrissake."

"You said 'might' and that's the correct choice of words," Vito said. "We know where the Schultz farmhouse is, but Sheriff Boyce isn't gonna send in a SWAT team and find the place falling-down empty."

"I think we should phone Joy and stop her from going in there blind. She's impulsive enough to do that, especially if she doesn't know what we know."

Vito said, "I'd go so far as to warn her not to go anywhere near that place without a heavily armed police escort. In fact, we should get in touch with law enforcement in that town and make sure they're aware of Sheriff Boyce's BOLO on Giorgio Luviano and Jennifer Hubbara."

It was clear as a bell to us that we had to find Jennifer and Luviano, our two murderous renegades, and put them in a cage. Sheriff Boyce's BOLO might help but so far it hadn't. I was on pins and needles about what might do next and I was even more panicked now that I believed it might come down on my daughter.

"If we get lucky they'll sign a suicide pact in their own blood and go through with it," Vito said. "They might think they're the new Bonny and Clyde, self-appointed killers of child rapists. The world doesn't understand them and they're doomed, so why not take themselves out."

"Romeo and Juliet re symbols of that syndrome too," I said. "Young star-crossed lovers forever sadly remembered. But sick as hell, if you really think about it."

"Are you putting down Shakespeare?" Vito jagged me.

"Hey, there were more bloody murders in *Hamlet* than in all of my movies put together."

"That's hyperbole," he said. "Maybe Joy will make a great find down there."

"If she doesn't get herself killed. I can't stop worrying, Vito. I have to phone her. I hope there's reception in those mountains."

"I don't think anything bad will happen to her. But hurry up and get in touch with her."

"I will, right now," I said.

But my call didn't go through.

Sometimes I wished I believed in prayer. But those days were long gone.

CHAPTER 30

The town library was only a few blocks from Miss Blue's Family Style Restaurant, and I walked there still tasting a ghost of the butterscotch pie and thinking how great it would be if Miss Blue's pies and cakes could be found in my neighborhood grocery stores like the ones by Marie Callender's were now, after being all the rage in L.A. for a number of years and then being franchised. Somehow her baked goods still managed to taste pretty great if you bought them frozen, especially the coconut cream.

The library was housed in a two-story yellow brick building with a glass show window where books were artfully displayed on an artificial grass carpet. I stopped to turn off my cell phone and saw that no screen was active, so I pressed the on button and still nothing happened.

Shit! No reception down here in the valley. If I could learn a bit more, I wanted to call Vito and my dad and give them an update, but I wouldn't be able to till I got back on the road. So, I dropped my cell phone into my purse and went into the library, thinking it previously must have been home to some sort of store-front business, maybe a shoe store or a hardware. I decided I very much liked it as a library. It was spacious and bright and the stacks and shelves were numerous but still nicely arranged for easy access. But I didn't browse. I went straight to the counter. There were two women at work behind it, one elderly and one much younger. I chose the older one as the likely English teacher, went up to her and said, "Mrs. Jefferson?"

She smiled and said, "It's miss I'm afraid."

It seemed she would say more, so I waited. She was a small woman with fluffy white hair, wearing a neat blue stay-pressed dress, a tiny watch with a slim golden band, no lipstick, no earrings.

She said, "I'm a spinster and I quite like it that way. Who wants to deal with unruly kids all day long only to have to come home and deal with an unruly husband."

"Good point," I said, smiling back at her. "I don't have any kids, thank goodness, and I got rid of my bitchy husband."

"Good for you. What can I do for you? I'm Mildred. It seems you already know my last name is Jefferson."

"Sherry in Miss Blue's restaurant pointed me in your direction. I'm Joy Cristi, a private investigator. I've come here hoping you can provide some information, Mildred."

I noticed that the younger librarian, an average looking brunette perhaps sixteen years old or so, in jeans and a Rolling Stones T-shirt, was paying more attention to me and Mildred that to the sign-out cards she was extracting from the inside packets of books and putting them back into a file cabinet.

"My gosh, a private detective?" Mildred was saying. "Who are you down here investigating for gosh sakes? I'm just a lowly English teacher and part-time librarian."

"Sherry mentioned that you taught the Luviano brothers. Dominic and Giorgio?"

"Is this about them? I suppose I shouldn't be surprised. I just hope they didn't kill somebody."

"Why would you say that?"

"Well, I can tell you some facts, and I can tell you some things I surmised about them, I suppose, Joy, but it will be up to you to separate the truth from the suppositions."

"I'm willing to do that if I might learn something important. Is there someplace more private where we can continue?"

"Actually there's a little office back here. Just come around the corner, behind the counter. Don't mind Octavia, she's just curious. We don't deal with very many strangers."

Octavia pretended not to pay attention to us anymore as Mildred opened a shellacked door and led me into the office. It was indeed small, but there was a gray steel desk with a gray folding chair in front of it. On the walls left and right there were thumb-tacked posters about the joy of reading, one slanted toward teenagers and one toward their parents.

Mildred sat behind the desk with her elbows on the blotter while I sat in front of her.

"Now tell me what's going on," she said. "Don't talk too loud. The door is hollow."

I said, "I'd be interested to hear what you may have thought about the Luviano brothers back when they were students of yours."

"Well, their IQ scores were pretty high, a little above average, but they were both under-performers. Dominic was two years older than Giorgio so I had him first, in my ninth-grade English class, then Giorgio came through. They held themselves apart from their classmates and didn't really try to make friends, and seldom did any of their classmates try to befriend them. It seemed they were totally antisocial. If either of them made any kind of friend for a little while, in a short time the kid who wanted to befriend them would get badly beat up by both of them. I tried to help them and so did the guidance counselor, with no luck whatsoever. I suspected they probably had bruises on their bodies because they both always wore long-sleeved trousers and shirts. But they wouldn't confide in us, if that's what was going on. In one of their guidance sessions, Giorgio blurted out he was scared of being sent back to the orphanage, but then he clammed up and wouldn't elaborate."

"Did they both manage to graduate?" I asked Mildred.

"Somehow they did, which for me was a wonderment, but I had to let it go. I knew they had the intelligence but I never thought they'd apply themselves toward a diploma. I don't think they could've bought their grades but maybe they stole copies of the tests somehow. But they would've had to steal a few different kinds of tests and for different courses as they passed from grade to grade. Even back then there were ways of cheating, like paying some other student to take a final exam for you. But where would they have gotten the money?"

"Maybe they were committing muggings or burglaries," I speculated. "Or shaking down other kids for their lunch money."

"Who knows?" said Mildred. "If any of my fellow teachers ever told me they were doing that I would've believed them. When they started going wrong, anything was possible."

"You mean worse crimes?"

She pushed back from her desk and said with baited breath, "There was a double murder back then. Two of them, in fact."

"Whoa, Mildred, you've certainly got my attention."

"Well, you've made me realize I can't keep quiet any longer, you see? Certain awful things have a history to them that I've never forgotten. When those two boys were still in eighth and ninth grade here in Hundred, a zealous young lady from Child Protective Services came to me one day, and she asked me if I could shed any light on how those boys were being treated by their adoptive parents, Barney and Helga Schultz. She said a neighbor believed they were being severely abused. Well, I thought about it and I had to tell her I suspected the same thing but didn't have any evidence, hust my own feelings. She was very disappointed to hear that said she would try to dig some more into it, but as time went by nothing came of the conversation, I had with her and I was sad because I thought something should have."

"You never heard anything more from her?"

"No, I wish I had. Because a couple years later, when the brothers were in their late teens, Barney and Helga Schultz disappeared. The boys stayed on at the farm with a lot of chatter going on around them, but no dead bodies were ever found and they never got arrested. Didn't ever get questioned as far as I know. And not long after that, two fellows who openly displayed their sexual preference for one another, before that was a wise way to be around here, got shot killed in their bed, shot a bunch of times with blood all over the place, is what I heard. Anyhow, that's when Dominic and Giorgio took off somewhere and to this day nobody can figure out where they went. All that makes me wonder why you've shown up in this one-traffic-light town all of a sudden."

It was my turn to take a deep breath as I contemplated how much I should confide in her.

I said, "I think I've got to tell you enough so you can keep yourself safe, Mildred, so here goes. If the Luviano brothers should come back here and you find out about it, stay away from them and phone the police. Giorgio and his girlfriend are suspected of committing a string of murders in and around Pittsburgh and Los Angeles."

"My God, that's worse than I could ever have imagined," said Mildred. "Don't tell me this is all about those movie people. We might be hicks, but we don't live in a bubble. We do get the news on television, believe it or not."

"Of course. I realize that, Mildred. I didn't come here to look down my nose at you. But please don't tell a soul who I am or what we've talked about. If Giorgio and his brother Dominic are killers, we don't want to spook them because that'd make them even more dangerous. If we can close in on them while they're none the wiser, maybe we can make them surrender without any more people dying. Including them."

"Oh my gosh!" Mildred said once again.

CHAPTER 31

I kept worrying about Joy while Vito and I were eating Primanti sandwiches in his office and washing them down with Iron City beer.

"Remember when this used to be called the baseball beer?" I said to him, trying to distract myself.

"Yeah, you felt like you weren't a real fan if you didn't drink Iron City. That was when Bob Prince and Jim Woods were the announcers and KDKA was the sponsor. Prince and Woods were great on the radio. They'd make the games more exciting than they actually were. They'd exaggerate the plays to make them more dramatic when the game wasn't on TV and nobody could accuse them of making stuff up."

"Then how did you know that's what they did?"

"Because I've got a good sense about baseball. I played second base in college."

"Did you ever win anything?"

"Nope. But I was a good hitter."

"How would I know if you're making *that* up? I never saw you play. You were an old dude and I was just a kid, ten years younger."

His cell phone rang and he glanced at the screen and took the call.

He said, "David's here with me, Sheriff Boyce. I'll put you on speaker phone."

The sheriff said, "We've got a possible sighting down in that town called Hundred, in West Virginia."

I blurted. "That's where my daughter is."

160

"It wasn't her that called it in, though. It was a farmer who lives down the road a piece from the place where the Luviano brothers were living after they were adopted. I hope Joy isn't foolhardy enough to snoop around on her own."

I said, "I keep trying to phone her, but either her phone is dead or she's got no reception."

"Well, fuck me," said Sheriff Boyce. "I'm gonna send a couple of my men. Cell phone reception is so bad the chief down there had to reach me on his land line. He was responding to my BOLO. But he's only got a six-man police force."

"You're saying he's fixing to follow up on the tip?" Vito said. "I almost hope he won't if he's that short of manpower and probably short of the right kind of weapons as well."

"You've got that right," said the sheriff. "I already asked him. He said he could put in a request to the West Virginia State Troopers for help, but they'd want to be assured that the tip is worth their time, not a dud in other words, so he's got to verify it first, if he can."

"You said you already sent two men?" I asked.

"Not yet, but I'm about to."

"I hope Joy is already on her way home," I said.

Vito glanced at me, knowing the sense of urgency I had to be feeling, and said to Sheriff Boyce, "How about if David and I get down there in a hurry? We could back up your two men. I could sign out some assault weapons and tear gas grenades from the police here in Clairton, and I already have two of my own riot guns."

"If you're gonna do all that, I think I should be there too," the sheriff said. "I'll head that way with my two men. We'll be well armed."

I said. "You don't know how grateful I am, Sheriff."

He said, "If this is a false alarm we'll end up looking like the gang that couldn't shoot straight, but I hope that's how it turns out."

Vito said, "I'll gladly wear some egg on my face so long as nobody gets killed."

"I hope Joy is on her way home." I couldn't help saying it once again.

"Try not to think the worst," said the sheriff.

CHAPTER 32

The librarian, Mildred Johnson, gave me directions to what used to be the Schultz place and I jotted them down on a sheet of notepaper because my cell phone still had no reception. "Did you hear about those new tracking devices that work off of satellite signals?" I asked her. "I intend to buy one for my car. Except it wouldn't work here, would it?"

"Don't ask me," she said. "I don't own a computer *or* a cell phone but I'm trying to get somebody to donate a plug-in computer to the library."

"Well, thanks for everything. Both of you," I said to her and her teenage assistant. "Just be sure not to tell anyone I've been here."

"We won't," they said almost in unison.

I said goodbye and left the building, walking toward my car. Then I almost totally froze when I had to pass a pickup truck with a rifle in the window of its cab and one of the guys I had seen at Miss Blue's staring at me from behind the wheel.

I almost retreated back to the safety of the library to wait till the pickup was gone -- but the other two guys rushed at me from a narrow alleyway and before I could grab my gun from my purse, one of them had me in a bear hug and the other one was choking me. The tail gate was already down when they pulled me in and slammed me down onto my stomach in the bed of the truck, cramming a gag into my mouth and tying me hand and foot with coils of rope.

Even in my terror I could tell they had done this kind of thing before -- probably more than once.

One of them slammed the tail gate shut and the other one held my gun up high enough so I could see it, and grinned as he threw my purse in on top of me. I heard the passenger door open, then slam shut after the two men got in. I tried to get my legs under me and stand so I could jump out even if I hurt myself badly by landing on concrete. I managed to get my right leg almost under me enough before the truck peeled out, burning rubber, and the sudden acceleration slammed me against the steel side of the cargo bed.

I realized that's all I was -- cargo. Cargo that was alive for now but would soon be dead. I had no illusions that I would get out of this alive. I had seen their faces and men like these would not let themselves be ratted out.

I could tell the truck was probably staying at near the 45 mph speed limit for a while on a smooth road, likely asphalt, not concrete, because that was all I had seen coming down here as I got closer to Hundred. I was aware of the likelihood I would not survive a tumble to the highway at that speed, but if I could stand up somehow and cling to the top side of the bed, and if my captors would stop somewhere I could risk letting my body hit the ground.

While they were going fast, with a lot of highway noise, I tested my ability to make some kind of scream in spite of the gag. But didn't sound like much. I couldn't get any volume past the gag, which was soaked with my saliva. But anyway, they never pulled over anywhere. They drove for I didn't know how many miles before making a lurching right turn that threw me hard against the side of the bed again., and now the road was narrow and rutted, or at least that's what it felt like. Lying on my back I could catch glimpses of overhanging tree branches.

Then the truck made a bumpy turn onto gravel which I heard clattering underneath. And finally it came to a stop, the engine was shut off and I heard the men jump down from the cab. Then one of them opened the tailgate and the other two dragged me out, dumping me on the ground. Which made them laugh.

"Nice trip, wasn't it?" one of the men said, and they all laughed again.

I heard somebody clomp down steps and twisted my head till I could see an aspect of a farmhouse as that somebody approached.

One of my captors said, "Your brother comin' out to see who we got here, Dombo?"

"He's sleepin'. Fagged out."

"From drivin' all night from Detroit?"

"No, from bangin' his honeybunch all night."

The men all guffawed as if they had just been hit with the punch line of a dirty joke.

I took note of the fact that Dombo had a black teardrop tattooed on his left cheek. He was wearing a wife-beater T-shirt and both of his arms were covered with bloody daggers, swastikas, SS insignias and an Aryan Brotherhood flag.

One of the men who had kidnapped me said, "What'll we do with this stupid wench,

Dombo? We hadda grab her when we overheard her askin' too many of the wrong kinda questions in Miss Blue's joint."

"Lock her in the barn. I know who she must be. Giorgio gave me the lowdown on her and two other detectives. Described her pretty good, too."

"Should we *carry* her down to the barn?"

Dombo snickered and said, "You ain't strong enough? It ain't very far."

Bending over and grunting, two of them picked me up bodily, one grabbing me by my trussed up feet and the other grabbing me under my armpits, and the third one leading the way.

165

When we went around the barn, where they dumped me on the ground and unlocked a side door, we passed a police car with two dead bodies slumped over in the front seat.

I understood immediately that if law enforcement had reason to take a look at whatever was going on here, and had dispatched patrol partners to do so, their effort had been thwarted.

When they didn't hear from the two who had been killed, would they do a follow-up? If so, I might stand a chance of being rescued.

On the other hand I might be used as a human shield if a gun battle broke out.

One of them used a key in a lock and hasp on the barn door, and when the barn door swung open they picked me up and dumped me on a dirt floor with a sparse coating of straw.

To my relief, one of them tore off my gag.

I said, "I have to pee." I really did have to, but mainly I said it in an attempt to buy a bit more freedom. If I could move around while I was all alone in there I might find a way to sneak out.

Thankfully one of the men untied my wrists and ankles and one of the others said, "Pee in one of the empty horse stalls."

"You're gonna be interrogated," the third man said. "Dombo or Giorgio will be comin' down here. Maybe both of 'em. Things'll go easier on you if you cooperate."

"Sure, easier," I said. "I already saw how easy it went for the two cops."

"You're startin' off on the wrong foot," one of the men said.

They all guffawed, then went out and I heard the lock being slid back on the hasp.

CHAPTER 33

Chief Walter Nichol was riding in the passenger seat of one of two official vehicles assigned to his six-man police force in Hundred, West Virginia. The Jeep SUV, basically black and white but painted with the town's logo, its dispatch number and the slogan PROUD TO SERVE & PROTECT, was being driven by Corporal Ray Benson with Sergeant Dick Ewalt sitting in the backseat. The adaptable third row of seats was not in use because it had been removed to make room for three bullet-proof vests and the only high-powered weapons readily available to them, two assault rifles and two Remington twenty-gauge shotguns, plus the kinds of ammunition those weapons required. Of course, they also had the 9mm Glocks that the department had issued.

A screen of steel mesh shielded the driver's compartment from the backseat, where felons usually sat in handcuffs, but since the screen was mesh, not solid, they could hear themselves pretty well in spite of tire and engine noise.

They were on the dirt road leading to what used to be the Schultz farm, conducting a surveillance. On their first pass-by they saw no activity and nobody outside in the yard or the adjacent field, so they kept going, not slowing down, knowing that they might be spotted yet not drawing any more attention to themselves than what was necessary by seeming to be headed somewhere else.

They continued in silence on the bumpy dirt road for another mile or so, then Chief Nichol said, "Turn around and go back."

Sgt. Ewalt said, "Nothing's happening, Chief."

"I'm not so sure yet," said the chief.

"Why don't we just go up on the porch and knock on the door?" the sergeant suggested sort of facetiously. "See who comes out, if anyone. If it's nobody who strikes us fishy, we can say we're selling raffle tickets for the Police Pension Fund. I even have some with me."

"Corny as that sounds, it might be our next step," Chief Nichol said. "But let's be patient first."

When they got the SUV turned around and backtracked a mile or so, the sheriff said, "Wait, hold back, Ray! There's movement down by the barn."

They all focused their attention and were stunned to see one of their police department's three patrol cars edging out from the right side of the barn. Two men were in it, one driving and one in the passenger seat, both heavily bearded, both in plaid shirts and coveralls with bibs and straps.

"Damn!" Benson snapped. "That patrol car is number two. Curly and Duncan signed it out this morning. Let's move on those fuckers and arrest them while we have the goods on 'em."

"No, hang back like I told you," Chief Nichol cautioned. "Let's see what they do."

They watched from a safe distance as their own police department patrol car kept on going.

"Should I let 'em get a lead on us?" Sgt. Ewalt asked.

"Yeah, but don't lose them. If they pull off into a field or somethin' we'll sneak closer on foot."

They felt helpless as the police car humped off of the narrow dirt road and onto the two-lane blacktop.

Chief Nichol said, "At least now we can keep up with them and probably not get made, long as we stay back enough and try to keep another vehicle or two between us and them. I just wanna see where they go. My bet is a gas station."

"That patrol car was gassed up and topped off when Curly and Duncan signed it out," Sgt. Ewalt said. "I guarantee you it ain't gonna need gas."

"Hold on. That's not what I was driving at," said the chief.

Sure enough, the patrol car pulled into the lot of a convenience store and stopped next to one of the pumps. The driver stayed put but the other guy jumped out, opened one of the back doors and grabbed a gasoline can. He used a credit card and filled the can up, put it between the seats again and jumped back into the patrol car, and it got back onto the blacktop road.

"They're gonna torch it," Benson said.

"Yep," the chief said.

"Then how're they gettin' back to the farm?" Benson asked.

"One of their cronies probably knows where to pick them up."

"Oh," Benson said, catching on.

Chief Nichol knew Benson and Ewalt were good cops, but Benson had a lot to learn yet. The chief was forty-one years old and normally did not have to deal with very much violent crime, but he didn't expect to ever be able to pay his family's bills without a struggle. His salary was $40,000 per year. Benson only got $24,000 and after five years would be bumped up to $28,000. Ewalt, being a sergeant, was being paid $36,000. It wasn't enough to risk your life for, yet today they were all doing it. The chief had a cheerful, reasonably attractive stay-at-home wife taking care of a healthy six-year-old son who thank God had no physical or mental defects, and he loved them both with his whole heart and wanted to be able to go home to them. He could tell that Ewalt and Benson were as scared as he was. Ewalt was divorced and had no children, but Benson had a nineteen-year-old wife who had recently given birth to a baby girl. Because of the patrol car they were following, without two of his officers in it, Chief Benson knew they were no longer alive, and he dreaded losing two more of them.

He asked, "Do we have binoculars?"

"Yeah, in the glove compartment," said Sgt. Ewalt.

CHAPTER 34

Vito knew how to get to Hundred pretty quickly by taking I-79 toward Waynesburg, Pennsylvania, then Route 18 toward West Virginia. "I've never gone all the way there," he said, "just to Waynesburg when I had a cop friend whose daughter went to W&J. I went with him and his family when she got her diploma. Washington and Jefferson University, a beautiful campus."

"What about the rest of the way?" I asked him.

"I looked it up because we're already pretty sure cell reception is spotty. From Route 18 we have to hit State Route 250 the rest of the way. It crosses the whole town. Once we get that far, we may have to ask for directions. Hundred High School is on Hornet Highway, wherever that is."

"Hornet Highway," I muttered, hoping we cou ld find it without being able to GPS it.

We had decided during our phone conversation with Sheriff Boyce while we still at Vito's office that the high school would be a good place for us to rendezvous with him and his officers. The sheriff had actually been to Hundred a couple of times, for what reasons he didn't say. He pointed out that a passel of heavily armed cops and detectives would shake up the whole town if they made themselves obvious, but if we arranged to assemble in the lot by the football field we'd attract little attention since school wasn't in session and football practice hadn't started up yet. I wasn't so sure it would go off without a hitch, though, because when I was a kid my pals and I would take advantage of the Clairton Football Field when the varsity

171

team wasn't on it to play pickup games of touch football, which we called "tabby pass."

"How much longer till we get there?" I asked Vito for the umpteenth time.

"You're getting on my nerves," he said. "Joy is gonna be okay, mark my words."

In quite a few other tight situations his hunches had worked out and I hoped this would be one of those times.

At the moment he was doing ninety, swerving his black Cadillac in and out and passing every slower vehicle, and making full use of his fuzz-buster.

CHAPTER 35

Joy heard scraping noises coming from the other side of the barn's side door, then two of her captors barged in, making the door swing wide behind them, teasing her with a momentary chance of getting away. She could plow into one of the men as hard as she could, dealing him a body block. The surprise and force of it might knock him back so she could get past him and make a run for it across the field toward freedom. But it wasn't a real chance. It would never work. She weighed a third as much as he did. And there were two of them. It would be like trying to get past two pro linemen. They didn't look nimble, but they were huge and beefy and without scruples.

One of them laughed at her for fastening her eyes on the opened door. He judo chopped her to the ground and kicked her in her stomach when she tried to roll over and crawl. Then he yanked her to her feet and got her in a bear hug, their faces so close she could smell his foul breath and the sour saliva in his beard. He held her close and laughed in her face while one of his henchmen brought in two folding chairs and set them up, facing each other, close to the empty horse stalls.

The first two oafs shoved Joy onto one of the chairs and wrapped coils of rope around her upper body to hold her upright against the chair back, then they tied her feet and ankles together. She didn't have much fight left in her. Her stomach and solar plexus hurt so badly from the kick she had taken that she wanted to curl up and groan, but the bindings wouldn't allow it. her captors didn't gag her so she figured she was going to be forced to answer questions. Then they would probably kill her.

But none of them sat in the chair opposite her.

Instead, Giorgio came in, with a leering grin on his face.

CHAPTER 36

The three policemen were surprised when the squad car they were following left the highway and pulled onto the dirt road that led to the Schultz farmhouse.

"What the fuck are they doin'?" young Benson whispered. "I thought they was gonna get rid of it."

"I'm sure they are," said Chief Nichol. "We'll catch them while they're busy and move in on them."

"Gonna take 'em by surprise," Sgt. Ewalt said, trying to sound confident, even with a tremor in his voice. Like the other two policemen, he had never dealt with bad-asses who had likely committed a series of brutal murders.

The squad car stayed on the dirt road for the next two miles, then humped off the road into a weed-grown field less than three miles from the farmhouse.

"What the hell?" said Sgt. Ewalt. "Are they gonna try to dump it this close to where're holed up?"

Neither of the other two cops answered him.

"Pull over and park further down," Chief Nichol said. "So they won't spot us. Then we'll get out and creep closer."

He almost took the binoculars out of the glove compartment and hung them around his neck, but he didn't think he'd be needing them, so he left them there. When he got out of the Jeep so did the two others, easing the doors almost shut without slamming them. They surreptitiously crept along the tree line for a short piece, then stopped where they couldn't be seen. They peeked as the squad car nosed into the patch of woods bordering the field.

Sgt. Ewalt said, "I was right all along. They're gonna torch it. They'll drive in where there's a big enough clearing so's it won't catch all the trees on fire."

"I don't know if they even care about that," said the chief.

"Why not? asked Corporal Benson.

"They might be about to get out of Dodge," Chief Nichol said. "A forest fire would be a diversion for them. But we can't let that happen."

"I wouldn't mind if they accidentally caught *themselves* on fire," said Corporal Benson. "Good riddance to bad rubbish."

"We don't know that our two officers aren't in the trunk still alive," the chief said.

"I doubt it," said Sgt. Ewalt.

They drew their police-issue Glocks, each with nine-round clips.

"What about the shotguns?" Benson whispered. He would feel safer with one of those because one shot, even if off-center, would knock a man down or kill him by blasting his torso to shreds.

The chief said, "Let's go. Don't let 'em light the gasoline. Keep close to the tree line so they can't see us till the last minute."

They didn't need to track the squad car by mans of the crushed-down weeds because they had already seen where it had gone into the woods. They advanced quickly but warily, holding their guns down along their thighs, then they halted and kept to cover when they came to the clearing where the torching of the squad car was underway.

"Soak it up good," one of the bad-asses said.

The other one was pouring gasoline from the five-gallon can they had filled at the convenience store. He finished soaking the floor and the backseats, then moved to the front.

Chief Nichol barked, "Hold it right there, fellas!"

The two bad-asses froze. They sneered but at the same time looked shocked to be caught by three uniformed cops pointing Glocks.

The guy who had been pouring the gasoline gingerly set the can down, but the other one pulled out a lighter, flicked it and tossed it -- and the squad car went up in flames.

The bad-ass who had lit the car up ran toward the woods but the one who had dropped the gas can turned into a human ball of fire and fell down, flailing and screaming and trying to crawl.

The three cops backpedaled away from the intense heat, and even while doing that the chief had the presence of mind to take aim and shoot, and the guy trying to make it into the woods fell into a tree, grabbed onto it for a few seconds, then went down hard.

"I don't hear any screams from the trunk!" Sgt. Ewalt yelled. "I think that's where they are, but they must've been dead, thank God!"

Corporal Benson vomited without bothering to go behind a tree. Some of what he expelled splashed onto his trousers and ran down the front of his uniform.

Chief Nichol said, "Listen up, Sgt. Ewalt. I'll stay here with Benson, get him calmed down and cleaned up best I can. I want you to get in the Jeep and try and see if the radio system works. If not, go to that convenience store where there's a pay phone and probably a landline. Call the fire department and get them out here before the whole damn scene catches on fire."

CHAPTER 37

Giorgio Luviano was in the chair facing me with a smug smile on his face. He wore a black T-shirt, black pants, a black leather jacket and black engineer boots and there was a black leather holster with a Luger in it suspended from a black ammo belt around his thin hips. His long black sideburns were as perfectly sculpted as they were when I first saw him leering at me, on his web page.

It still seemed weird to me that such a badass wannabe had pipe-stem arms. If he had built them up a little, he would've had more room for his ghastly tattoos.

He said, "Cheer up, cutie pie. I might let you live. We're destroying all the evidence we were ever here. Poof goes the squad car and poof will go the house and barn before we cut out."

I said, "Where's Jennifer Hubbara?"

"She's in the house. You two might leave together when I get done with you. She's innocent. She never killed anybody. She deserves to have a nice life. She's barely getting started on what promises to be a terrific career. Her millions of fans aren't gonna wanna see her gettin' put in jail. She's a minor. She's not responsible for whatever the cops think she did."

"You're trying to make me believe you pulled off a whole series of well planned murders on your own?"

"I don't care whether you believe it or not, it's the truth. I'll be long gone when the police

take her into custody They won't be able to hold her after she tells them her true story."

178

There was no doubt in my mind that he was lying, trying to protect his teenage femme fatale. In fact she was more to blame than he was. She was the instigator and the mastermind. He was her boy toy, her favorite psychopath. She had him wrapped around her little finger. He was going to protect her even if he went down. Could that be their plan? And could they actually think it would work? I couldn't help thinking of the soul-smothering jury nullification in the O.J. Simpson murder case.

Giorgio continued his twisted rant. "I want you to have all the right information to tell the cops, Joy. I've already written a full confession that leaves Jenny out of it so she can take it with her. You'll be her corroboration, so I want to let you ask me anything you want. But she'll have a gun on her in case she gets the idea you're gonna turn on her."

Did he actually think that harebrained scheme was going to work? Perhaps it would, if Jennifer ever went before a jury. She wasn't a topnotch actress but she could probably make the tears flow and sway at least one juror -- or even all twelve. Could I believe that Giorgio would set me free so I could shore up Jennifer's testimony if it came to that? Maybe, maybe not, but it was my only hope. I had to play along. Which meant I had to pretend to be skeptical at first, then allow myself to give in little by little till I convinced him I was a convert to his spiel.

"Okay," I said. "I'll grant you one thing. Jenny was likely molested by her own father and that's what drove her over the edge. It might gain her a great deal of sympathy but not enough to fool a psychologist and land her an insanity plea."

"Plea to what?" Giorgio shot back at me. "I'm telling you she's innocent. She never murdered anybody."

"And I'm telling you I need proof. The cops are going to tell her the same thing."

Angrily, he said, "You're prejudiced against her."

"That may be so," I conceded. "But if you committed all the murders on your own, you'll have to tell me -- or Jenny will have to convince the cops and the prosecutor."

I could barely believe I was playing a mind game with this psychopath. A mind game I couldn't afford to lose.

"Okay, the first one," he said. "The first one was that fat-cat movie guy, Lance Goldman. Jennifer told me what the big action star, Blaze Stewart, had been doing to her ever since she was a child. It really pissed me off and I said I would kill him for her even if I went to jail. But that's not what she wanted. Instead she said Mr. Goldman had to die and that didn't make any sense to me, till she said he was gonna rat out her father."

This stumped me. I said, "Lance had the goods on Derrick Hubbara? How did that happen, Giorgio?"

"Because of Jennifer's mother, Leona. She told Mr. Goldman on Derrick and demanded two million dollars from his studio or she would file a case on him and Derrick both. A case like that would incite public outrage and destroy their cash cow, the biggest grossing movies they ever made, the Blaze Stewart franchise. But Jennifer also believed the whole mess would destroy her career when it came out. I told her it'd probably just make her more famous, but she didn't think so. She thought about killing her mother. But I talked her out of it."

I said, "Why was she so fixated on Lance Goldman? Even if he were dead, Leona Hubbara could still extort Derrick. It would've made better sense to kill Lance and Leona both, right at the outset."

"We didn't intend for Leona to live all that long. We decided we needed to put some space between her murder and Lance's."

"Okay...but you had to pull off a double kidnapping and murder and get it in motion at a crowded airport."

180

"Hey, I got guts!" Giorgio said vehemently. "And I'm good in the sack. Wanna try me?"

I didn't even want to think about it.

"Besides," he said, "I'm a hardened killer, as the news media would say. Me and my brother Dominic already killed four people when we were living right here."

"Okay, I guess I believe you," I managed to say. "I can buy into your motive where Lance Goldman was concerned. But why did you kill Darby Coltrane?"

"Well, we were both victims of abuse and once we started killing it felt right to keep on with more good deeds."

"You said 'we'. You and Jenny? A Freudian slip? I'm supposed to believe you were acting alone, Giorgio."

"I didn't mean me and Jenny, I meant me and Dominic."

"I didn't think Dominick -- or Dombo, as you call him -- was ever in Hollywood. Was he?"

"No, he didn't have nothing to do with Darby Coltrane. But here's one he worked with me on that you don't know nothing about. Derrick Hubbara is dead. I don't know if anyone has found his body yet. It's in his exercise room."

This particular bolt out of the blue shut me up while I contemplated it. If he had an accomplice, it might not have been Dominic. So I said, "That sounds like a motive for Jennifer, not you or Dombo. She'll inherit, won't she? If you can keep her out of prison."

"Don't get smart with me or I might decide not to turn you loose," Giorgio said.

CHAPTER 38

Without as much difficulty as we anticipated, Vito and I located Hundred High School on Hornet Road and met up with Sheriff Boyce. He was driving his country police vehicle with two more county cops in the passenger seats, and he also had recruited a SWAT team travelling in a camouflaged U.S. Army surplus transport big enough to hold a dozen men and obviously heavily armored.

Sheriff Boyce said, "I obtained arrest warrants for both Giorgio Luviano and Jennifer Hubbara. The warrants were signed by a Pennsylvania judge, so I don't know for sure they'll hld up here. But Chief Nichol told me he'd have West Virgina warrants. We're covered if they make a run for it, so long as they don't go west, into Ohio."

Vito said, "Correct me if we're not on the same page, but it seems to me that you and your men should lead the way and David and I should follow."

"I agree," said the sheriff.

Ever the quipster, Vito said, "That way there'll be less chance of my Cadillac getting shot up."

The situation being what it was, nobody cracked a smile. Not even Vito.

It had to be one of the unusual caravans ever deployed in these parts: An Allegheny County Sheriff's Jeep from Pennsylvania, a military-type assault vehicle full of armed men in full body armor, and a flashy black Cadillac lagging behind. I felt like I was part of a powerful posse that would probably be able to overcome any force going up against us, but that didn't mean we wouldn't take casualties. And Joy might die if she were to be used as a human shield. I was so overcome with worries about her that I was unable to think straight. Were we going to find her? Was she here or not? And if so would she be alive or dead?

After twelve miles or so in our strange convoy, we turned off the blacktop onto a dirt road and Vito said, "Gotta be the one that leads to the Schultz place, David. I think this is where the suspense ends."

I wished he hadn't put it that way.

Our convoy went about six miles on the dirt road, then Vito and I smelled a heavy, tarry smoke coming from somewhere. We couldn't see much of what was ahead of us because our view was blocked by the large armored vehicle. We could kept our eyes peeled to either side of the Cadillac but still couldn't make out where the smoke might be coming from. But the convoy stopped after coming upon a Hundred Police vehicle to one side of the dirt road. Again, Vito and I, with our limited view, were not aware of the discovery at first. Then when the armored vehicle moved up a little, we saw the police Jeep parked at an angle that would've helped conceal it from a field and a patch of woods.

"Let's get out. We're sitting ducks here," Vito said.

As we swung our doors open we saw that a big red Hundred Fire Department truck was parked on the far side of the open field with part of it nosed into the edge of the woods. The acrid smoke we had been smelling was coming from back among the trees.

"Looks like whatever was burning, the fire has been put out," Vito said.

Just then three uniformed policemen with pistols drawn came into view, approaching us from across the field and the patch of woods where the fire truck was nosed in and smoke was still coming from. We immediately figured the uniformed men for the captain of the Hundred police and two of his officers. Sheriff Boyce stepped forward to greet them and Vito and I moved in closer. The SWAT captain came forward too. There were quick introductions among all of us. The captain of the Hundred Police Department was Walter Nichol and his two officers were Sgt. Ewalt and Corp. Benson. The SWAT officer was Captain Ortiz.

Chief Nichol said, "We're in some deep shit here. I don't know how many assholes are holed up at the farmhouse with the Luviano brothers, assuming they're actually there. David, we don't have any knowledge that your daughter is there either. But we've got to move in on them. They killed two of my best officers and burned them up in the trunk of their own squad car. We killed the two who did the burning, but they may not be the same ones who did the murders."

"A lot of unknowns," Sheriff Boyce said. "We'll be going in blind. We don't know how many we'll be confronting, how well they're armed and how much heavy firepower they might have."

"Well, like it or not, we had better proceed briskly," SWAT Captain Ortiz said. "Right now we might have the advantage of surprise. But we won't have it much longer. Especially if they come looking for their dead buddies when they don't show up at the farm."

"Right now they're showing up in Hell," Chief Nichol said.

"Where they belong," said Sheriff Boyce.

"One of 'em already got his little taste of Hell," Sgt. Ewalt said. "He burned himself up setting the squad car on fire."

I noticed that Corp. Benson, who couldn't have been older than in his early twenties, still looked queasy from the things they had already gone through.

184

CHAPTER 39

We approached the farmhouse on foot after working our way toward it through the woods. We didn't want to make easy targets of ourselves in the open ground. Chief Nichol and Sheriff Boyce told me and Vito to hang back and let the SWAT guys do what they were trained for. I didn't want to look like a coward, but what he said made sense. I saw that Even Chief Nichol and Sheriff Boyce were deploying themselves behind the SWAT team.

Vito said to me, "David, you find a big fat tree to hide behind and don't move out of the woods till this is over."

"What about you?"

"I'm not gonna be braver than I have to. But I'm smart enough not to take the lead."

"So am I but I can't totally cop out. My daughter is probably in there."

"What if we rescue her but then she finds out you've been killed. Think about that, David."

"Don't worry, I *am* thinking about it."

"If I stay here, will you stay?"

I didn't respond quickly enough because the SWAT team was already on the move. In a matter of moments, they were going toward the farmhouse in military assault fashion. There were eight of them, four in their armored vehicle and the other ones spread out four on each side of it, crouching low in a half trot, armed with assault rifles.

It would've tough for me and Vito to catch up to them now, so we stayed put, and eaten up with suspense.

Sheriff Boyce, Chief Nichol and their officers were advancing in the lee of the assault vehicle, armed with pistols and riot guns.

With all this firepower going into action, I dreaded that Joy might become collateral damage. I tried to take heart from the fact that Sheriff Boyce was carrying a megaphone, which told me he would likely call upon the occupants of the farm to surrender. If they took heed, maybe there wouldn't be any more bloodshed.

CHAPTER 40

Giorgio got up from his steel folding chair, leaving me tied up in mine. He didn't pull out his Luger and I hoped it meant he wasn't going to shoot me...yet.

Then Jenny Hubbara came into the barn through the open side door. I had been told she was here, on the farm someplace, but I was still shocked when she made her appearance and gave Giorgio a kiss. She was in jeans, a black T-shirt and black boots like his, and she also sported a Luger in a black holster on her hip, with a black ammo belt, like his, and it made me think of a true-crime series that I used to watch on TV called *Murderous Couples*. It was hosted by a woman who had been an FBI profiler for twenty years, and after she had narrated the heinous crimes of the perpetrators she was profiling, she never tried to over-analyze them, but simply said, in almost every show, "They did it because they wanted to."

I had little doubt that Giorgio and Jennifer would be a perfect couple to be portrayed in that vicious true-crime series. They were truly evil taken either singly or as a duo, yet I had to continue acting as if I had fallen for Jenny's so-called "innocence" as depicted by her boyfriend.

Did they really believe I was so gullible?

Jenny came over to me and said, "I'm so glad you're going to be sticking up for me. With you and a good expensive lawyer on my side, I'm sure we'll be able to convince a judge and jury. I trust you not to turn on me, Joy. And to prove it I'm going to be the one who unties you."

I knew her proffered trust in me would be superseded the moment I made an ill-advised move. Superseded by high-powered round, or several rounds, from her Luger. I thought it wise to thank her, and I did so with a smile on my face. I held still while she untied the knots and loosened the bonds around my wrists and upper body. Giorgio looked on approvingly. He didn't even have his hand on the butt of his gun.

"How many followers do you have here?" I asked in an off-handed way.

He said, "Not so many as you'd think, Joy, but we're going to grow. I have to launch a serious recruiting effort for our cell. Jenny is the sold beneficiary of her father's estate, as well she should be after all he put her through. She'll finance me and nobody will be the wiser, after she turns herself in. There are five guys and four women in the house playing cards, getting stoned and packing up to get --" He froze in mid-sentence -- then blurted, "Where the fuck are the fuckers I picked to get rid of that squad car? They shoulda been back here by now, shouldn't they?"

Just then a voice from outside blared out and I was as startled as Jennifer and Giorgio.

"ATTENTION! COME OUT OF THE HOUSE AND THE BARN WITH YOUR HANDS ON YOUR HEADS! YOU ARE SURROUNDED! THIS IS YOUR LAST CHANCE! SURRENDER OR BE KILLED!"

Giorgio drew his Luger from its holster, but Jennifer didn't. She put her hand on his arm.

Just then gunfire erupted, at first just a couple of shots -- but then a horrendous fusillade.

I thought some of Giorgio's henchmen must have come out of the house shooting only to be mowed down in retaliation. At least that's what I hoped. And it seemed to be confirmed by the ensuing silence.

Then I heard my dad's voice.

"Joy! Where are you, honey! Are you here!"

"Don't you dare answer him!" Jennifer warned me.

Giorgio yanked me to my feet and I staggered and almost fell because my ankles were still bound. He said, "I'm goin' out there, Jenny! If they shoot at me I'll plug this babe in her pretty blonde head!"

"No, they'll kill you, honey!" Jenny cried out.

"No, I think they'll let me surrender. I'm gonna find out, but Joy will be my protection. They won't shoot at me if I hold her close."

CHAPTER 41

The SWAT team killed five of Giorgio's neo-Nazi henchmen but three more, two women and one man, never came out of the farmhouse till they surrendered and were taken into custody. So were Jenny and Giorgio and Giorgio's brother, Dominic.

Joy and I were crying when we fell into each other's arms, and Vito wasn't completely dry-eyed either. But our happy ending wasn't even an ending yet.

The aftermath of a crime spree is the tough part: putting the pieces back together dealing with the lives that have been ruptured.

Jennifer Hubbara and Giorgio Luviano were indicted. Dominic, also known as Dombo, was held for several weeks while Chief Nichol supervised a backhoe crew that dug about fifteen or sixteen deep exploratory holes all over the Schultz farm without discovering any buried bodies. It couldn't be proven that Barney and Helga had been murdered, so neither Dominic nor Giorgio could be charged for whatever had been done to the Schultzes. Both brothers were relentlessly grilled on the topic but did not crack. Sheriff Boyce and Chief Nichol desperately wished to charge Dominic for *something*, but to their surprise he didn't have much of a rap sheet from his time in Florida, so they concluded that he had either kept his nose cleaner than anyone would've thought or else he had cleverly avoided detection for any serious crimes he may have committed.

True to his word, Giorgio confessed to all of the murders he and Jennifer were suspected of, and insisted that he had acted alone. The police and the prosecutors in Pennsylvania and California did not believe him but there really wasn't any hard evidence against Jennifer and it seemed she would get off scot free unless Giorgio flipped on her. But she had turned over the letter he had written in hopes that they would help absolve her, and she also swore that my daughter Joy had heard all the "honest and true" details of the murders from Giorgio himself while she was his captive. To Jennifer's chagrin, Joy did not deny hearing all that but told the authorities she hadn't believed a word of it.

Since Jennifer Hubbara was only fifteen when the murders went down, her highly paid attorneys fought to have her prosecuted as a juvenile. As part of their strategy, they had her voluntarily submit to several psychological evaluations, which enabled them to waste time, on the principle that justice delayed is justice denied. They filed lots of pre-trial motions on top of every other delaying tactic imaginable, and the upshot was that the poor little teenager anguished in a Pittsburgh jail for almost two years. Meantime it was deemed that the crimes she was accused of were so heinous that she would be tried as an adult. Her bail was set at two million dollars, while the news media and public opinion surveys railed against the judge and the lead prosecutor for coddling her.

Sheriff Boyce and one of his ace detectives kept on visiting Giorgio Luviano in Western Penitentiary and putting pressure on him to testify against his former teenage lover, but he kept refusing and insisting he had acted alone. Meantime, Jennifer kept sending him letters reminding him of her "undying love and devotion." Sheriff Boyce read every letter before they were delivered to Giorgio in his cell, in hoped that she might write something that would implicate herself -- but it never happened. He decided that she might crack if he could get something on her, and he put her under surveillance and within a few weeks the round-the-clock stake-out resulted in footage of her checking into a motel with a young man who had been an assistant cameraman on one of her father's movies. Pleased with himself, Sheriff Boyce paid another visit to Giorgio at Western Penitentiary and showed him the surveillance footage on a laptop. But Giorgio still didn't crack.

A week and a half later he was found unresponsive in his cell, with a swastika carved into his forehead. A coroner determined that he must have used a jailhouse razor to cut the bloody Nazi symbol into his own flesh, which was pasty white in death.

Shortly after that bizarre development the chief prosecutor decided not to pursue charges against Jennifer Hubbara any farther. He held a press conference to announce that there was not only an absence of direct evidence against her, but the inmate, Giorgio Luviano, who might have been her accomplice, had killed himself in prison.

In the aftermath, Vito and Joy flew to Los Angeles to meet with Veronica Goldman to personally convey their sympathy for the way things had turned out and explain why there was nothing more they could do about it.

"That little bitch gets to go on with her life and her career!" Veronica exclaimed bitterly.

"I have a hunch she won't last long," Vito told her.

"You think someone will bump her off?"

"I think she's a sick puppy. No one will want to cast her in anything anymore and she won't be able to deal with it when she's knocked off her high horse."

"What goes around comes around," said Joy.

"Comes around and hits *me* in the gut," said Veronica. "How am I supposed to deal with that? I wish Jennifer Hubbara nothing but the worst."

"Maybe time will heal," Joy said. She didn't normally deal in platitudes so she had to force herself.

"Veronica smiled to show as if she was joking when she said, "Maybe I should cozy up to her, let bygones be bygones, and cast her in a prestigious supporting role to show her I mean it. Then set up a fatal accident on set."

"If you do that," said Vito, "you'll be adding to the string of murders that were so hard to solve."

"You solved them but that little bitch ended up free as a bird!" Victoria snapped back at him.

"My final bill is due," he told her. "I gave you a ten percent discount."

For more information on John Russo,
his books, movies, and official merchandise,
please visit:

www.TheJohnRusso.com

ABOUT THE AUTHOR

With 40 books published internationally and 19 movies in worldwide distribution, John Russo has been called "a Living Legend." He began by co-authoring the screenplay for the horror classic, *Night of the Living Dead*, and went on to build an iconic decades-long career.

His books on the art and craft of movie making have become bibles of independent production and have won a national award for Superior Nonfiction. Quentin Tarantino and many other noted filmmakers have stated that Russo's books have helped them launch their careers.

John Russo wants people to know he's "just a nice guy who likes to scare people" -- and he's done it with novels and films such as *Return of the Living Dead, Midnight, The Majorettes, The Awakening, Heartstopper,* and *My Uncle John is a Zombie!* He's had a long, rewarding career, and he shows no signs of slowing down. In 2024, Lionsgate acquired a Western written by him, *The Night They Came Home*, about the murder spree perpetrated by the Rufus Buck gang, who were all hanged in 1895.

Russo's popularity among genre fans remains at a high pitch. He appears at many movie conventions each year as a featured guest, and hundreds of attendees come to his tables or to the bar to share drinks, jokes, and serious conversation.